Becks
A ROCKSTAR ROMANCE DUET

THIA FINN

Becks
A Rockstar Romance Duet, Book One
Thia Finn

ALL RIGHTS RESERVED. This book contains material protected under the International and Federal Copyright Laws and Treaties. **Any unauthorized reprint or use of this material is prohibited.** No part of this book may be reproduced or transmitted in any form or by any means, electronic or mechanical, including photocopying, recording, or by any information storage and retrieval system without express written permission from the author/publisher.

FILE SHARING: Please note that this book is protected under the Digital Millennium Copyright Act (DMCA). It has been made available for your personal use and enjoyment. **No permission has been granted to upload this book onto ANY file-sharing websites.** Doing so is a violation of federal laws and measures have been taken within this file to track the originator of such shared files, should it be found on piracy sites. Thank you for respecting the hard work of the author to produce this content.

WARNING: This is a work of fiction. Names, characters, businesses, places, events and incidents are either the products of the author's imagination or used in a fictitious manner. Any resemblance to actual persons, living or dead, or actual events is purely coincidental.

Disclaimer: The material in this book contains graphic language and sexual content and is intended for mature audiences, ages 18 and older.

Edited by Swish Design & Editing
Proofreading by Swish Design & Editing
Book designed and formatted by Swish Design & Editing
Cover photo model: Jamieson Fitzpatrick
Cover photographer: CJC Photography
Cover image Copyright 2018

ISBN 13: 978-0999292372

Copyright © 2018 Thia Finn
All rights reserved.

Dedication

People come in and out of our lives for a reason. In this world of authors, I have met many wonderful people who have encouraged me, helped me, worked with me, and befriended me, and I'm the better for it. So, to these people, I dedicate this book. Because without you, there might never have been a Becks.

Prologue

"Take your lying, cheating, miserable fucking ass out of my house, you ungrateful little shit." He raised the menacing cane over his head ready to hit me as he'd done so many times in my life.

"I've never lied, cheated, or begged you for anything in my life. The only damn thing I'm ungrateful for is the fact that no one else figured out you killed my mother. Maybe not with a gun or a knife, but with your fucking words and your hand. You, the big man of the county, were too concerned that others might see some of your real damage on her beautiful face to hit her with your fists where it showed. And you were too much of a fucking coward to fight with a real man."

"That's because I'm the only real man who ever lived in this goddamn house. You and that half-breed brother of yours call yourselves men, but the truth is you're nothing but pieces of shit trash. I found your mother and pulled her up from the garbage, but she never crawled out of it. She only bred whelps who had that in them, too. Now get the hell out of here and never come back."

A glass of whiskey sliced the air close to my head and smashed into the wall behind me.

Scorching heat burned my neck. I glanced over my shoulder to watch flames shooting skyward, but they didn't cause my steps to falter. This day had been coming for years, but I never dreamed it would end in fire.

The distinct rumble of a Harley's motor sitting idle only lasted for a short minute before roaring off in the opposite direction I traveled. It carried the only living relative I knew of. Konan rode the machine hard if the pop, pop... pop, pop... pop, pop sound of the two pistons hitting so quickly was any indication. The fading sound said my brother grew closer to the edge of the county and further away from me.

Once more in our lives, we moved. This time we were on our own, though. We'd done it so many times before that calling someplace home seemed like a dream. I knew this dream would have far different outcomes than the others. Those dreams haunted me day and night because that's what nightmares did.

A smile ghosted my lips until I heard sirens wail in the distance, the noise causing my body to rattle as it grew closer. When the sound blistered my ears, I stopped to watch the manned truck barrel toward me. A red blur sped by. Men and women holding on grew anxious as their adrenaline rose with each mile passing in the direction of the fire.

I feared for them as I always did when I heard the distressing call of a public service vehicle. Those people put their lives on the line each time they drove away from the station. I admired them for the servants they were. Their bravery amazed me because I knew I didn't have what it took to sacrifice myself the way they chose to daily.

Walking backward down the side of the road leading to Main Street, I watched the firetruck turn the corner for the last time before the driver slammed his foot on the brakes to stop at their destination.

I knew what they would find.

I knew how it would look.

I knew what they would believe.

My legs moved faster and my heartbeat raced, carrying my guitar case and a backpack. Escaping the scene was my only option until the truth could be proven. My life held change I hadn't planned on so soon. Now the choices were taken from me.

NEWS REPORT ONE

Reporter: This is Janna Alfred reporting for *Channel 8 NEWS*. I'm here at the home of Beckon Masters, who has yet to be accounted for at this time.

Anchor: Janna, have you been able to speak to the fire chief yet?

Reporter: No, these brave men and women haven't stopped their valiant efforts to save this old home. As you can see, the structure is completely engulfed in flames. It looks like the fire chief might be able to answer a few questions now. Chief Batson, what can you tell us about the fire at this point?

Chief: The home was completely covered in flames when we arrived and looks like it will be a total loss. The firefighters have been working nonstop to try to contain the fire. It was too far gone when we arrived to do any more.

Reporter: Can you tell us if the house was occupied?

Chief: No, not yet. We'll make a thorough sweep of the home once the fire's completely out. It's burning too hot for any of my team to enter.

Reporter: Thank you, Chief Batson. This is Janna Alfred reporting live from the northeastern part of Lawback County.

Anchor: Thank you, Janna. We will hear more from you when more information is available.

BECKS

"Get your lazy ass up and let's roll. We've got things to do, dipshit."

"Shut the fuck up. I just got in bed." Rolling over, I took the pillow with me to cover my head and filter the noise.

"Oh, hell no. We've got work, and you're earning your keep, remember?" My supposedly generous landlord, Kody, refused to let it go. When I found myself on the floor, trapped between the bedframe and the wall of the closet-size room where I slept, I knew my day wasn't starting the way I'd planned.

"Okay, okay. I'm up, asswipe." The mattress landed with a thud back on the bed. Something wasn't right about being rolled out of a nice soft bed.

Becks

"Damn right, you are. Thanks to me. Now get your clothes on and come eat. Work's waiting and we're burning daylight." I watched his booted feet stomp through the doorway from under the bed before I crawled backward to the foot and made my way clear of the bind he'd left me in.

My body stayed deprived of sleep. The job took up my days and playing my guitar took up my nights. Kody told me more than once that sleep was overrated. He didn't have a night job, so I couldn't understand how he knew what he was talking about. Lies, all lies.

I staggered to the kitchen table with one eye closed. Bacon and eggs waited on a paper plate. Rolling them in a slice of bread, I grabbed my coat and a bottle of water and took off for the truck before he left me behind.

The big job waited on us thirty miles away. Thirty extra minutes of sleep sounded great but so did eating some breakfast. For the labor we provided, I needed to keep up my energy. Before I took this job with my friend Kody's dad, doing manual labor sounded like a foreign language. Being on my own forced me to do whatever it took to support myself. Musician jobs hadn't panned out on a regular basis yet.

I liked to eat and sleep in a bed so using power tools provided what I needed to do both of those. The bang of a hammer or the whirr of a saw sounded like a paycheck these days. Kody's dad, Randy, allowed me to work even though I had no experience. Apparently, finding trustworthy helpers didn't happen too often. I could be that guy.

"Boards coming down. I'm through here," Randy yelled from the second floor. The framing contract he secured stated we would frame the entire subdivision of two hundred homes. Knowing Randy, though, bids were out in a fifty-mile radius for new locations when this one ended. The suburbs of Nashville exploded with growth about six months ago, and it didn't look like a halt to progress was coming anytime soon.

Unused items on this job would be taken to the next one, so I gathered each one and loaded them on the trailer since my job description included loading and unloading. I never realized how lax my muscles were until I started this work. My arms ached for days in the beginning.

After a month of picking up eight or ten-foot two-by-fours and lifting them over my head to hand up to the framers, my arms started taking on a whole new look. I didn't need a gym to define my biceps, they toned up like never before. Ripped muscles appeared in the mirror when I bothered to notice.

Becks

The day ended when Randy said so, and since he paid by the hour, no one argued with him. He liked to knock off by five on Fridays which made us all happy since we had weekends off. The job paid well, and I banked all I could and still get by. When I left this place, I planned to have enough to live for a year without worrying where my next meal would come from.

My guitar called to me every time I walked back through the door in the evening. I found gigs when I could which were usually every Friday and Saturday night. Weeknights I practiced all different types of music. I learned to play by ear, but I taught myself to write music as a teenager. Writing music made me more marketable so through sheer determination, watching YouTube, and working with other musicians, I learned. My next life would be as a successful musician.

We finally loaded up for the evening and headed back to the house. Kody and I found dinner where we could, but I stayed away from fast food. The more my body toned up, the more I wanted it to. I'd never been a gym rat, but I knew the ladies liked a ripped body. I was willing to do anything to make myself more appealing when I struck out on my quest to be a musician, I gave it my all.

"What are we eating tonight?" Kody asked as we rumbled down the road in the backseat of his dad's work truck.

"It's your turn to decide."

We both turned as the police car passing us flipped on his siren. The shrill sound scared the shit out of me. It took me back to that night. No one here knew anything about where I came from, so I had to keep my fear under wraps.

Every chance I found I rolled into the city and looked for a gig. Kody became a life saver when I met him a few years ago while playing at a bar with a small band. He stood off to the side watching the singers. The band hired me on the nights when they decided they needed some backup guitars, so the lead singer could basically show off for the women. Since I played just about anything, they hired me often.

One night during a break, and I jumped off stage to get more water, Kody started talking to me about being in the band. I explained I wasn't part of it just a hired guitar player filling in. Not being able to carry a tune in a bucket, Kody's dreams as a singer drifted away on the off key tune he sang for me. My ears bled from the experience, but he was passionate about everything he did, and I couldn't help but like the guy.

This time when I came into Nashville, my mission carried a different end result. I planned to stay, something I'd never done before. Kody showed up while I played a set. He bought me a beer during my

Becks

break. I mentioned needing a steady job, and he told me about his dad's company, and just like that, I became a framer's helper with a new friend.

"You guys would be so much better off if you cooked your own food," his dad offered from behind the wheel.

"Yeah, but who would clean up the mess?" Kody told him. "I sure as hell ain't washing dishes."

"No." I joined in. I had washed so many dishes in my life, but some things were best left unsaid.

"Bunch of pussies," he whispered. "Kody tells me you're Mr. Guitar Man over in the city." Randy's eyes met mine in the rearview mirror. "You any good?"

"Hell yeah, he's good. Works every weekend at a different place. He plays with some of the best bands," Kody threw out before I had time to reply.

"Why do you play with different bands? They won't keep you?" His dad's line of questioning made me nervous. *Maybe the musicians didn't think I was good enough.*

"I play where I'm needed, filling in for bands who hire me to take the place of someone who's sick or has a conflict."

"Can't you stick with one band? Seems like a waste of time to play around that way," Randy continued, but I wanted this conversation to end, like yesterday.

"Pops, quit hassling Becks about it. Maybe he likes it that way. He gets to meet a lot of bands and learn a bunch of good songs and different music, and then there's all the women." He punched me in the arm. "He's gotta direct line to all the pussy he wants."

"I've yet to see one single woman walk into y'alls' house. Either he's ashamed to bring them home, or he ain't getting any more than you are, dipshit." The old man started laughing until it turned into a coughing fit. He's old enough to know those cancer sticks he smokes all damn day are going to kill him eventually.

Kody looked at me with worry about his dad. When he finally started to breathe again, Kody shrugged his shoulders. "When you going to throw those fucking cigarettes away, old man?"

"Shut up, boy. I'll still be around to see you move out of my rental house." He glared at his son over the seat. Nothing else was said until we rolled into the driveway. The rental house sat on one side of the drive with the main house on the other. We both paid him rent from each check, so we never worried we wouldn't have a roof over our head.

Kody and I gathered our jackets from the day and headed to our own house.

His mom stuck her head out the door, "I got supper ready if you two want to join us tonight."

Kody looked over and raised his eyebrows in question. I nodded. "Heck yeah, Mom. What are we having? Never mind, we'll eat whatever you've cooked."

Becks

"Clean up, and we'll sit down when y'all get here." She closed the door behind her.

"Why'd you even question her? Her cooking is better than anything we can buy."

"Yeah, and she won't charge us." He slapped me on the back. "Gotta love my mom."

"I love her already, and I hardly know her."

That admission of love for his mom caused my mind to drift back to times in my home where I wished for a warm, caring person like Kody's mother. I remembered a time when my mom loved my brother and me. Those memories vanished at some point though, probably shortly after the mean bastard brought us home again in a police car.

My father sat in the front seat smoking a stinking cigar. Being the county judge, he thought he could do whatever he wanted and pretty much did. When my mom ran with us the first time, I remembered nothing because I was too young. Konan had a year on me, so he couldn't have any thoughts stored away of the judge.

The next time she ran though, we both knew why. We helped all we could at four and five. The bruises on our skin told the whole story. Our mother stashed grocery money away for months so our escape would work this time. A friend from high school gave her a car with car seats so the police wouldn't know who passed them on the road.

Konan and I rode and slept in those restraints forever. At least to us it seemed that way. She stopped long enough to put gas in the car and let us go to the restroom. She chose stations that only had outside doors to them so the attendant couldn't see who got out of the old silver car.

We finally stopped when we reached a place that had mountains all around. It had recently snowed, and that was definitely something two boys remembered. She put coats and gloves on us at a motel and let us go play in the playground covered in the fluffy white stuff. When we started shivering as the sun went down, we ran to the room, and she made us hot chocolate and canned soup for supper in the little microwave the room had in it.

We stayed there a few days but moved on, and on, and on.

Negative thoughts fell away as I stepped into the shower. The hot water Kody left me had a definite lukewarm feel about it, but I didn't care. I stood letting it run through my hair. My hair needed cutting sometime soon. The dishwater blond fell well past my shoulders. The length caused me a lot of heckling at work, but the women loved it when I got on stage. Since it hung longer than any of the other band members I sat in with, that's how they referred to me when they yelled suggestive ideas on stage.

Becks

The front men or lead singer in each band captured the most attention, and I tried to remain as anonymous as possible. Most of the bands wanted it that way. Hell, some asked me to wear a bandana or mask to cover my face. I hated this, but I needed to work, so I tried not to voice my opinion of being covered. Since I would never be an actual member of their band, they didn't want their fans to know me. I understood their thinking, but I didn't have to like it.

"Hurry up, dude. Pops is probably having a coronary over there waiting on us."

"All right." I turned off the water, dried, and dressed. Kody waited at the door for me when I stepped out.

Kody leaned over and sniffed me, and I pushed him off. "What the fuck?"

"Who are you trying to impress smelling like that? You take a bath in cologne?"

"No. I got a show, and I need to leave as soon as we get through eating."

We stepped through the doorway to a delicious aroma.

"Damn, Mom. That smells great. Is it roast?" He leaned in and kissed his mom on the cheek as she stood at the farm sink.

"Yes, and now that y'all are here, we can sit down." She glanced over her shoulder at Randy, who helped himself to the mashed potatoes. His plate seemed overloaded to me before he dropped the heaping spoonful. "Your dad couldn't wait." Mrs. Richards rolled her eyes with her back turned to him.

I grabbed the chair where I occasionally sat, not wanting to disrupt the flow of things that were arranged long before I came here.

"I blessed it the whole time I was cooking, so fill your plates. At least I know you boys get one good meal a week when I invite you here."

"Mrs. Richards, you don't have to feed us. We get by pretty good on our own, but I appreciate the invitation. The food all looks and smells wonderful."

She laid her hand on my arm. "I know I don't, Becks, but I like to know someone's enjoying all my hard work. Lord knows Randy never comments. It's more like a grunt."

Kody started laughing, and I looked over at him. She seemed sincere in her comment to me, but he thought it funny. "Mom, he's been grunting like that as long as I can remember."

Randy never stopped eating. Guess that was his way of showing appreciation for the wonderful meal she treated us to.

Kody dove in as though someone would steal it from him. It amazed me how this father and son ate. It reminded me of the ditchdigger on the property where we worked. They scooped it up and shoveled it in.

Remembering the times as a child my knuckles received a rapping from the backside of my mother's butter knife and then scolded and sent to my room hungry, I learned table manners fit for any formal state dinner. My parents never allowed anything less. I placed my napkin in my lap and noticed Kody's still folded beside his plate.

"You ain't gotta be all formal here. My parents don't care about that shit."

"Kody, please don't talk like that at the table."

"Leave him alone, Annette. He worked a hard day today and deserves to be left in peace to eat his dinner." Randy never looked up from his food as he spoke to her.

It took everything I had to not say something to this man. He treated me like one of the guys from the beginning. Never questioned what I did unless I did it wrong. He took the time to teach me what I needed to know on the first day, so why did he treat his wife like she was the maid and stupidly requested her son eat like an adult. I kept my head down and ate my meal without saying a word. If me keeping quiet made her life easier, it was the least I could do.

Letting his poor treatment of his wife wouldn't go without question though. I had to pick my time to ask when it was better for Mrs. R. I noticed Kody finishing off the last bite on his plate and quickly ate the few remaining on mine. He stood and took his plate to the sink, rinsed it and stuck it in the dishwasher, and I followed his lead. At least someone taught him to do something for his mom.

"Oh, Becks, you're our company, you don't have to do that."

"I don't mind at all. The meal was delicious. Thank you for having me."

"Suck up," Kody said as he passed between his mom and me.

Randy stood and took his water glass to his recliner in their den, an extension of the dining area. Their home looked recently updated. I supposed with him being a contractor, they needed to stay on top of styles changing.

"Y'all going down to Broadway tonight?" the old man asked us both. I hadn't answered to another adult about my coming and going in several years, so the question caught me off guard.

"Yeah, Becks has a show at ten. I'm going to watch it and drink a little beer." He looked at me grinning. We hadn't discussed him coming with me, but I didn't care either way.

He knew I lived to play gigs, but he worked as a damn good wingman. The oversize man-child sized up the women while I performed, so all I had to do was show up at the table when the set wrapped. This worked well, especially if he could find two lookers who came together. We'd spent many nights banging chicks in the same apartment and left before sunup. Neither of us were looking for anything long term, so it turned into a win-win situation.

NEWS REPORT TWO

Reporter: This is Janna Alfred. I'm here at the remains of the home of Beckon Masters. As you can see, the home was gutted by the recent fire. Today, Chief Batson is here with Arson Investigator, Dan Halloway. Mr. Halloway, what can you tell us about this investigation?

Mr. Halloway: Not too much yet. Several caseworkers are here today to try and come to a conclusion whether the fire was intentionally set or not.

Reporter: Are there indications this was arson?

Mr. Halloway: Too soon to tell. In old homes like this, the wiring is almost always faulty. This house was built in the early 1900s and doesn't appear to have had any type of renovations to the electricity in the home in quite some time, if ever. It'll take some tracing to see if we can pinpoint the origin of the fire.

Reporter: So, no conclusive evidence at this time.

Thia Finn

Mr. Halloway: No, I'm afraid not.

Reporter: Chief Batson, did your unit find anything of note in the home?

Chief Batson: I'm not at liberty to say at this time.

Reporter: What about the owners? Have they been accounted for?

Chief Batson: Two bodies were found in the rubble. No names are being released, pending identification by the next of kin.

Reporter: Thank you, Chief and Mr. Halloway. You heard the Chief. The bodies haven't been identified yet, so this remains a mystery as to who was found in the home. This is Janna Alfred reporting from the northeastern part of Lawback County.

Chapter 2

BECKS

With my guitar case, I maneuvered my way backstage after waving to Bryce, the manager. He stood behind the bar watching the bartender draw beer from the spigot. Paige worked hard on her nights to tend bar at Tapped. Kody introduced me to her the first time we came in. She looked young in the dim lights, but he quickly let me know she was out of our league, being older than us by several years.

She didn't put up with any shit from the regulars who sat at the bar. What she did, though, was listen. Not once had I heard her voice an opinion about something one of the drinkers told a crazy story about.

Sitting at the bar was Kody's thing. He enjoyed gazing on the various customers who drifted through.

Not me, though. I played my guitar each time we walked through the door.

Kody always started the evening sitting across the bar from Paige drinking a few beers, so he had an opportunity to get to know her better than me. He liked listening to the people who stopped in after work to grab a beer before heading home. I'd asked him if he was planning on doing something with all those stories, but he shook his head and claimed he wasn't listening. I knew better because he would repeat the best ones to me on the way home.

We'd arrived a little earlier than usual tonight, and I planned to spend the time going over the song list I'd been given earlier in the week. A surprise waited for me when I opened the door to the backstage. A naked ass pumped into a dark-haired woman trapped against the wall across the room.

"Shut the fucking door," the lead singer of the band I planned to sit in with yelled. "Stay in or get out, I don't give a fuck but keep the damn door closed."

"Uh. I..." The sight caught me off guard, so when I glanced at the woman's face, and our eyes connected, indecision struck me whether to stay or leave.

Her arms were loosely draped across his shoulders, and her expression seemed bored with the entire situation. I looked down to see jeans and lace lying on the floor below them. She made a moaning noise, and I glanced back up to find her still drilling me with her dark eyes.

Becks

The singer pushed her hard against the wall, and she grunted out another sound so fake, I knew she wasn't into the sex and was ready for it to be over. How could he not tell it since her mouth spoke directly in his ear? "Oh, honey, that's sooo good."

I couldn't help myself when my eyes rolled, and a smile slightly lifted my lips. I grabbed the doorknob and turned it making another noise.

The woman yelled out before I could slip through it. "Don't leave now, sugar, the fun's just starting. You can come over here and join us."

Shaking my head, I walked out and pulled the door closed. A drink before the show had my name on it now, something I rarely ever did, but after that sight, tonight would be one of those nights.

"What's going on? Thought you were going to spend the time practicing," Kody spoke between the last few gulps of his beer.

"I'll have what he's having." Paige nodded at me.

"Something got you rattled?" Kody wouldn't let it rest.

"Nothing."

The door I'd escaped through opened, and the lead singer walked out alone heading straight to the men's room. He tipped his head at me when I looked at him. If that was supposed to be a message that it was my turn, he was completely mistaken. The last thing I wanted was anyone's sloppy seconds. I'd had my fair share of threesomes but not that way.

"You have words with the band already?" Kody continued.

"Nope, didn't say a word to him."

The beer mug slid across the bar top at me, and I took a long drink from it. Someone sat down on the stool next to me while the glass still rested against my lip. Before I looked, I knew it was the woman from the room. *Damn, how did I get into shit like this?* All I wanted to do was play my guitar and sing.

"Hey, darlin'. You want to buy a girl a drink?" Her voice grated on my ears.

"No." No way was I getting involved with this woman.

"Thanks for nothing." She spun around on the barstool and huffed off toward the exit.

"She must have been desperate to come looking for you." Kody laughed.

"Not so desperate that she offered for you to buy her a drink."

This came from Paige, and I laughed so hard I almost fell off my stool. Kody didn't find it funny. He saluted Paige and took his beer to a table.

"I think you insulted him."

She glanced his way and then looked back at me. "He deserved it. He comes in here and sits around like he's some big player commenting on all the women he sees. I rarely see him leave with one. Even if he likes their looks."

"Maybe he thinks he's not their type."

Becks

"He has a type?"

I smiled at her. "I guess. Never thought about it."

"Looks to me like if they walk, talk, and have a vagina, they're his type." She wiped the bar down where his mug left a sweat ring. "What about you? You have a preference?"

The seats in the bar were now filled, and I scanned the crowd. "No, not really, but then I'm not looking for anyone either."

"What are you looking for?" She leaned back against the counter behind her flipping the bar rag around.

"I'm just trying to play my guitar and get better. I came to Nashville to make it."

"You and every other musician in the Northern Hemisphere." Her cynical mood made me take a hard look at her. Was she always like this?

"Let me ask you the same thing then. What are you trying to do? You plan to tend bar the rest of your life?" My question surprised her, and she turned away and got busy filling a drink order shouted at her from down the bar. Watching her lean over the counter to get a bottle from the cooler, I admired the small peach shape staring at me while I took the last sip of my beer.

"You staring at my ass, pretty boy?"

"Just admiring the scenery." I stood. "I'm still waiting for your answer, but I have to go play some music. You know, what I came to Nash to do." I winked at her and threw enough cash down to cover my drink, including a generous tip for her and moved off to practice.

The other band members trickled in as I continued rehearsing the songs for the night. This band would never hold my interest. They played for the money and not for the love of the music. Audiences here at Tapped enjoyed them, but with the number of bars in Nashville hosting live music, no one usually stuck around longer than a set. Bar hopping became a way of life for most of the people who visited. The band knew it. Hell, I knew it, and I hadn't been here that long.

Taking the stage at exactly nine o'clock, we launched into the first song of the night. I played back-up to the lead guitar which was fine by me. Once in a while, they would allow me to play a solo, and I would show the crowd what I could really do. Playing the songs they chose, in their rhythm, bored me to tears some nights, but when they would give me a chance to shine, I took it. We never knew who might be in the audience to discover new talent.

Tonight must have been my lucky night because after the first set ended and we took a short break, a tall, thick guy came close to the stage where I sat guzzling a bottle of water.

"Hey, kid."

Now there's a name I hadn't been called in a while.

Becks

"Yeah?" I glanced at him over the top of the last sip of liquid.

He looked around to see who might be listening. I could have told him no one cared in this place. When he looked back at me, I knew he meant business.

"You're not part of this band, are you?"

I hopped down off the stage to look him in the eye. My height wasn't intimidating but looking at someone eye to eye when you met was important. I liked things on even footing, and since I had no idea where this conversation might be headed, standing on the same playing field seemed like a better plan.

"No. I'm sitting in for their backup guitar player tonight. What can I do for you?" I watched him as he reached into his pocket and pulled out a card to hand me.

"I'm Ethan Shandell. I work with 13 Recordings." He stuck his hand out, and I gladly shook it.

"Becks O'Donnell, Mr. Shandell. Great to meet you." My smile relayed messages to the moon.

The man looked around the crowded, noisy room. "Give me a call, and let's set up a meeting time next week."

My hand nervously flipped back and forth over one end of the card. "Sure thing. I'm looking forward to it." Part of me wanted to jump up and down and make girly noises, but I kept my cool and smiled at him.

"I think the band is ready to start the set."

Thia Finn

Glancing around to the stage, all the other members were picking up their instruments and the lead singer shot me a death glare. "Yeah, I guess they are." I extended my hand to shake his again. "I'll call Monday morning, Mr. Shandell." He shook my hand, nodded, and turned to leave the venue.

Paige looked at me from behind the bar. Her genuine smile told me she knew what Shandell wanted. He probably stalked the bars regularly looking for new talent. I was probably one of many he handed cards out to but right now, the high I floated on made me want to jump over the bar and kiss that smile of hers into the next millennium.

The club filled with customers tonight, and we played three more sets before it shut down. Exhausted but too excited to admit it, I packed away my guitar to go home.

"So, what'd the suit want?"

"Huh?" Two ripped jean knees stood on the other side of my case.

"What'd the fucking guy who gave you a business card want, dumbass?" The same guy banging a woman in the back room looked down at me. I'd done nothing to piss him off during the night, so I wondered where the angry tone had come from. Tonight's show had to be one of my best, so I knew it didn't have to do with my performance.

"Oh, uh. He gave me his card and told me to call for an appointment. That's all he said to me." Why did I bother giving him an explanation? I owed him nothing, but he owed me money for tonight.

"Just like that? He wants to meet with only you?"

The fasteners clicked closed on my guitar case before I stood and looked at him. "Yeah, that's it." His glare said he wanted more information.

"Why didn't you say we came as a group?"

Staring back at him, I needed him to get the message. "Why the fuck would I do that? I'm not part of this band. You hired me for the night. Nothing more."

"Yeah, but our group made you look and sound even better, so you should have told him we came together."

"Not the way I see it." Someone stood behind me now. This scene could get ugly fast if the rest of the band saw things this jerkwad's way.

"What's going on here, Becks?" Kody's voice gave me a reason to breathe a little easier. Fighting never topped my to-do list, but I wouldn't back down, even if it involved the whole band.

A slow, deep voice sounded over all the drinkers still finishing their last call of the night. "Y'all boys got a problem here?" The bouncer from the door stood tall in front of the stage.

The lead singer glared at me and then turned to look at the tattooed biceps bulging from the sleeves of the big man's shirt.

"No, man. We're good. Right, Seth?" I directed my question to the man who had originally approached me.

He smirked and spun around to look at his friends. "Yeah, we're good. Let's go, guys. We've got some shit to discuss about tonight's show." He glanced back over his shoulder at me. "Seems like we're going to need to find another backup guitar player that knows how to fucking play for real. Becks' playing tonight sounded like amateur hour. He's just not up to our standards. Brought our whole show down to a lower level."

The bouncer, Tevo, Kody, and I stood there listening to him spout off bile. We all knew Seth talked shit but let them go. The last thing I wanted to do was go to jail for fighting in a bar, especially after the great night I had.

Tevo looked at me. "You good, Becks?"

"Yeah, great."

"What's got the royal asswipe worked up?" I grinned at his term for Seth.

"A guy from 13 Recordings gave me his card. Wants me to make an appointment with him. Seth saw us talking and got jealous." Laughter shot out before I could stop it.

"Yeah, that dude's going nowhere. He can barely sing much less play guitar." He pointed his finger at me. "Now you... you're the real deal. You don't need to be working with that bunch of chumps anyway. Move

Becks

on to a better band. Hell, form your own band. You're good enough."

"Thanks man, appreciate that." We clasped hands, and he patted me on the back. "Get on out of here. Make something good of yourself."

"Yeah, I'm trying to. Every chance I get." I grabbed my case, and Kody followed me out to his truck.

SOPHIE

"Thank y'all and goodnight everybody. Come see me again. I'm here Thursday through Saturday." The microphone carried my voice across the listeners as they made their way back to their tables from the dance floor. My energy wasted on the cover songs I played, I packed up my guitar and then my laptop.

The trusty Apple played all my background music in the small club. I couldn't afford to hire more band members since I only took a cut of the door. My Acme Feed and Seed job paid the rent. With all the hopeful musicians who came to Nashville to be discovered, I prayed daily for having the paying job. One slip-up and someone stood in line to take my place at one of the best paying clubs in the city.

Becks

Cover songs of country music paid my other bills since that's what people came to Nashville to hear, but my heart longed to play the alternative rock music I preferred. I sang that for myself now but one day, one day... I let my dreams float away on the wind as I finished packing up to go home. Two a.m. ended my set, but my body buzzed from the time on stage.

The bus stopped around the corner from the small venue I played. Racing out to catch the next bus home to the east side of Nashville, a seat waited on the empty bench at the stop. This rarely happened but at this time of night, it made me happy to see it. The workers who closed the bars never left as early as I did from a gig, but the patrons who took advantage of mass transit did.

Footsteps caused me to glance up. Two men walked toward a truck parked in the lot across the street. I'd seen the one carrying a guitar case before. His long, dark blond hair made him impossible not to notice. A close-up look never happened since our meetings always happened after dark. All I could see was the dark t-shirt he wore stretched tightly across his chest and arms. Naturally, he worked out. Probably a gym rat by day.

I'd met my fair share of them who came into the club and Acme. They loved hitting on me, but I never took them up on an offer. Harmless flirting made for higher tips at Acme, but that's as far as it went. The last thing I needed was some meathead hanging around waiting for me to get off work. Pepper spray rested in my hand on my keyring, and using it was my first line of defense.

As a female with one hand carrying a laptop and a guitar across my back, I might have been easy prey to some. Anyone brave enough to try to attack me would find a fight on their hands because backing down had never been my style. With the brothers I grew up fighting, I had a good chance of holding my own, for a short time anyway.

The door locks popped on a truck and Mr. Muscles loaded his equipment in the back while the other man stepped in and started the loud vehicle. Ugh, men and their trucks. Was this one to make up for his little-dick syndrome? I laughed to myself.

The sound must have carried across the empty lot because I watched the musician turn his head in my direction before he stepped up in the passenger's seat.

Shit, had I laughed that loud? The two sat in the truck with the Mr. Muscles looking at me longer than necessary. *Please don't let them be talking about me.*

The truck turned and headed across the mostly empty parking lot in my direction. I rolled the pepper spray around in my palm making it ready to shoot straight. The monstrosity slowly came closer which gave me more time to grow anxious. It pulled to the side of the bench, and the window went down.

"Uh, we noticed you sitting here by yourself. Don't you think that's dangerous? I mean, we're not trying

Becks

to scare you or anything, but it's dark out here and you're all alone."

Staring straight ahead, I said, "Nope. I'm fine."

"Well, if it's okay with you, we're going to wait here in the truck until your ride comes."

My head jerked around to glare at him. "What?" I yelled. "Why would you do that?"

"Because you're out here in a deserted parking lot on a dark street after two in the morning with the drunks all leaving the bars. Neither of us thinks this is a safe plan for you or anyone really. I know I wouldn't feel exactly safe sitting alone."

"Yeah, right. I'm sure you'd be quaking in your boots." I sat back on the bench. "Do whatever you want, but you don't need to stay for me. I'm good."

I heard them talking to each other in a tone so low I couldn't understand them. *Please don't be planning to kidnap me.*

"We would ask you to let us take you home, but given the fact you're clutching something in your hand and you say you're fine sitting there, we're just gonna turn off the motor and wait with you."

"Whatever. It's your time you're wasting." My eyes blinked as I stared into the darkness, so I wouldn't have to look at them. The truck cab was too dark to see into, so I couldn't make out their faces, and making eye contact with them made me feel more vulnerable.

"So my name is Becks O'Donnell, and this is Kody Richards."

"That's nice." No way was I telling them my name. "Why are you telling me this?"

"I don't want you to be afraid. We're only trying to help a fellow musician."

"Well, thank you, but really, I'm fine. I do this several nights a week."

"You sit out here on a bench alone in the dark several nights a week? You got a death wish or something?"

"No, but it's cheaper to take the bus than drive my car, so this is what I do. I don't need your permission, you know." My tone should have told them to leave, but they didn't take the hint.

"Right. Well, like I said… we'll wait here until you're gone."

It seemed like the minutes dragged by as I checked my phone for the time. The bus would be at least five more minutes. At this hour, they usually kept closely to the schedule.

"What club do you play in?" He continued to try and make conversation when he could shut up and leave. Didn't he realize the two of them sitting there made me more nervous?

"High Five Bar."

"Oh, I know that place." He looked toward the bar that sat at the opposite corner of the block. "At least

Becks

you're not walking too far to your bus every night. I guess that's a plus."

"Look, dude. I don't need or want your approval for what I do or where I go. I'm sitting here minding my own business that you and your friend are trying your best to climb into. He can start his big-boy toy and go home. I'll be fine." Wishing I could actually see his face when I finished my rant, I watched him hoping it would drive home the point and they should leave. No such luck.

"You're right. What you do is none of our business, but I couldn't live with myself if I found out you'd been hurt while sitting here, and I did nothing to help you. I'll stop asking questions, but we aren't leaving until you take a seat on the bus."

"Fine."

"Damn right, it's fine."

The sound of laughter from the other man filled the night air. I couldn't tell anything about him with the darkness surrounding him inside the cab.

"Hey lady, you're the only woman I've ever met who's more stubborn than Becks."

"Not talking, remember?"

"No, Becks said he wasn't asking any more questions. He said nothing about me talking."

My head whipped around to look past the long, blond-haired man. "So, he asks questions, and you talk. The two of you make a great pair. Y'all use this scheme with the ladies all the time?"

"No," the two yelled at the same time.

I heard a loud roar coming down the street as a bus lumbered along carrying its passengers through the night. Happy that I would be one of them, I stood and gathered my bag. Before I stepped closer to the curb, I looked back over my shoulder.

"Thank you for waiting with me." Mr. Muscles nodded and rolled up his window. I made my way to the second seat to sit where I always did. Glancing out the window, I watched the truck pull away. Just like he said, they left once I sat down. *Hmmm, guess there might be some good men still left around.*

The doors whooshed closed before the bus pulled away from the curb. As the truck pulled around in front of the bus and sped away, I smiled.

The old me would have climbed in that truck in a heartbeat, but the new me held onto caution. The old me would have prayed they followed the bus to where I lived. The new me kept a smile for a few minutes over them driving away.

The new me was a winner at life. The old me lost life a long time ago.

NEWS REPORT THREE

Anchor: Now for news around the county. We reported on a fire that claimed two lives in the northeastern part of Lawback County. Our field reporter, Janna Alfred, has been following this story for us. Janna?

Reporter: Yes, thank you, Lisa. As you remember, fire gutted the home of Beckon Masters and his wife. I've been following this story for our viewers since that night. I'm here today with Dan Halloway, who's the arson investigator for the county. Mr. Halloway, what can you tell us about this fire?

Mr. Halloway: This scene was a tricky one to investigate. At first, we suspected arson for several reasons, a gasoline can be being one of them. With further investigation though, it looks like the fire didn't start with an accelerant but with a lit cigarette.

Reporter: So, you're ruling the fire an accident?

Mr. Halloway: No final ruling has been made yet. We still have a few more areas we plan to look at more closely.

Reporter: Can you tell us about the casualties from the fire?

Mr. Halloway: Yes, two bodies were found in the upstairs bedrooms. Pending notification of next of kin, we will be withholding names.

Reporter: Isn't it suspected that the two bodies were the homeowners?

Mr. Halloway: No comment.

Reporter: Is it safe to say the homeowners haven't been accounted for, and they are both older people?

Mr. Halloway: Yes, this is true information.

Reporter: There you have it. The home was a total loss, as you can see from the rubble. The homeowners, Mr. Beckon Masters and Mrs. Laura Masters, are unaccounted for, and no clear ruling has been made on arson or accidental start to the fire.

Anchor: Thank you, Janna, for that report. (turn to audience) We will keep you posted as news develops at the scene.

Chapter 4

BECKS

"I can't understand why women put themselves in that position." Kody turned down the radio. "She's a sitting duck on that bench alone at that time of night, just waiting to be taken."

"Yeah, me either, but she sure as hell didn't like us telling her what we thought." I pulled the business card out of my pocket, turning on the overhead light so I could put the number in my phone. "Some people don't see danger or don't want to believe bad things can happen to them."

"That's stupid thinking in my book." Kody wasn't ready to let it go.

"Maybe it's the only way she can play her music and survive in this town. If she's here alone, then it probably is."

"She needs to find some friends then because she's going to find herself in a situation with guys not as nice as we are."

A bark of laughter left my lips. "I bet she wouldn't find you so nice if you met her in a different place."

"Hey, I'm always nice to the ladies. You know that."

"Right. Let me think back on that some." I rubbed my hand across the stubble forming on my chin. "What about Becca? You weren't exactly nice to her."

"Becca was a different case."

"You're so full of shit."

We both laughed as he drove us back to the house.

"Thanks for coming in, Becks." Mr. Shandell shook my hand. This man was all business here in his corner office of the twenty-story office building.

"Happy to be here, sir."

A smile spread across his face. "No need to be so formal, Becks. Sir reminds me of my old man."

His clothes may have spoken high dollar, but his friendliness made me feel at ease. Coming in this morning created a lot of anxiousness on my part. This could be the chance I prayed for.

Becks

Flipping through a file on his desk before looking back up at me, he leaned back in his plush leather desk chair and steepled his fingers. "Tell me about yourself, Becks. I want to get to know you."

"Well, uh... I'm from a lot of places. My mom moved around often." He didn't need to know we ran from creditors every time my mom got behind on her bills. "I taught myself how to play guitar when my friend's dad gave me one."

"He gave you a guitar?" His eyebrow lifted with the question.

"Yes, sir. Mr. Thomas was a great guy. He played with some local bands, and if I was at their house hanging out, and he pulled his out to practice, I couldn't stop watching his fingers move over the strings. The look on his face as he sang words to songs I'd never heard before held my attention like nothing else."

When I stopped and took a breath, Shandell leaned forward in his chair. "Was he any good?"

"He was the best in my eyes. Of course, I was only about ten at the time. I couldn't be still to save my life. Stayed in trouble in school, but his son was my best friend, so Mr. Thomas thought me learning to play would keep my hands and mind occupied."

"What about his son? He play, too?"

"No. Tom had more problems than I did, but it didn't bother me. I'd moved three times that school year so keeping friends was hard to do." I looked at

Thia Finn

Shandell trying to decide how much he needed to know about my life. He nodded to me as if he understood what I was trying to say.

"Anyway, Mr. Thomas had an old guitar he said he didn't use anymore. It was a small one that I wondered if he'd bought for Tom who never learned to play it. Tom's motor skills were not quite right. He had a stroke at birth, and his mom refused to stick around and help him learn, so it was just him and his dad."

"Did this man teach you to play it instead?"

"He started to and then my mom made us move again as soon as school was out. I tried to give it back to him before we left. He refused to take it. Said I needed it a lot more than Tom did, and I should practice every day."

"Well, from what I saw, you must have taken his advice because your skills are some of the best I've heard in a while. I'm assuming you taught yourself."

"Yeah, I got lucky. When we moved into the next apartment, the high school band director lived below us. I'd sit on the steps at night and play around with the few chords I knew. He'd see me there every day, and I guess he grew tired of the three chords because he brought me a guitar book with songs in it. The illustrated chords above the music showed me how to make them with my fingers."

"So you did teach yourself."

"Mostly, I played by ear, though. After I got those chords down, I could pretty much play whatever I heard."

"You only play by ear, then? No reading music?"

"Yeah, I can read music, too. The band director brought me a lot of beginner's books, and I learned everything they taught in them. He let me take them when we moved again. Playing the guitar was the only thing I was ever good at. I decided that if I was meant to be a musician, I better learn all I could to be successful."

"That's quite a story, Becks. Sounds like you were meant to be a musician. Do you sing or compose?"

"I've written a lot of songs, a whole book of them. I can sing, but the bands I play with never need a singer unless it's a little backup. Nothing much to talk about."

"I see you brought your guitar." He nodded at my case resting just inside the doorway. "How about you let me hear one of your own songs."

My guitar spent all day Sunday in my hands. I practiced every song, every riff, every chord I knew. The idea of playing my own music was more than I could ask for, but I hoped he would. The opportunity to show my talent to someone who could make things happen for me lay at my feet. I hoped he liked the one I loved the most.

Thia Finn

We sat together hand in hand
Listening to our favorite band.
Her beauty always captured me.
The love we shared came like a breeze.

Easy come and easy go.
My life keeps on changing
And that's one thing
I will always know.

Take my heart baby, hold it safe
Store it with your best keepsakes.
The dust might gather before I return
Remember us when you long to burn.

Easy come and easy go.
My life keeps on changing
And that's one thing
I will always know.

And that's one thing
I will always know.

The last chord faded off slowly with my voice. I'd
written this song when I fell in love the first time. A
pretty girl told me I looked hot when I played my
guitar, so naturally, I played for her both times I saw
her. On Monday, I was in love, and she was walking
with another guy to class. That was the last broken

heart I had in school. Girls proved to be a lot of trouble.

Shandell stood as soon as I finished. "You're absolutely right, Becks. You can play and sing. With a little tweaking, that song could be your first hit." His smile said it all.

"You think so? I mean, I've not recorded any music."

"Don't worry about recording. We'll get you into a studio with a band behind you. The full sound a band adds will make it richer. "Audiences like a unique style they can identify with. You have the ability to bring that. Let's get you into the studio this week. What day can you come in to work with the band?"

I sunk back in my chair letting out a long breath. My paycheck was important and leaving Kody high and dry that way wasn't right. This could be a problem for me.

Mr. Shandell looked up from the tablet he studied on his desk. "What's going on Becks? Is recording your music a problem?"

"I work from at least eight to five, weekdays."

"Right, right. I understand, but this is important for your career. Can you get into the studio after five? Musicians work anytime. The day you record, though, we're going to need you here earlier and probably for more than one day."

"Coming in later isn't a problem. I'll have to see if I can take off a couple of days in a row, though."

Thia Finn

"I'm sure you'll work it out, Becks. This is the beginning of what could be a great career in music. Don't you think you deserve to give it a try after all the effort you've put into your music?"

Shandell's intense stare told me he meant business. It wasn't an ultimatum, but I knew he would want me twenty-four seven if this panned out.

"Yes, sir. I do." I stood and offered him my hand in agreement.

"Great. Great. Let's get this moving forward then. I need you in here on Wednesday evening at seven, and we'll go from there. You can plan on Thursday and Friday evenings as well. We look at scheduling first of next week to see how many evenings you'll need.

"Sounds good. I'll talk to my boss about taking the days."

"Listen, Becks. I believe in being honest with my clients. New talent rolls into Nashville seven days a week, all looking for the same thing. You've got a sound worth working with, or I wouldn't have asked you here today. I know you've sacrificed to get where you are, and now isn't the time to back away from your dedication. It's the time to up it, to stretch it for all you're worth. You get what I'm saying?"

"Yes, sir. I get it, and I'll do what it takes. It's all I've ever wanted."

"Then let's do this thing."

Shandell shook my hand, and I knew this was the beginning of something bigger than me. Something I'd dreamed of for so long. Something a fire or a nightmare couldn't hold me back from. I only hoped Randy felt like he could let me go. I hated letting the guys down, but I'd been saving money for this exact reason. Guess I'd be using it until I got a paycheck from 13 Recordings. Hopefully, that would be soon.

As I drove up to the job site, I practiced my speech to Mr. Richards one more time before I got out of my old truck. I prided myself on being an honest person because fucking liars made me hate people. Being honest with my boss could go either way, but at least I'd walk away with my dignity.

"Glad to see you decided to join us, music man," Mr. Richards yelled down from the second story rafters he finished up on. "I'm coming down for a break so wait there."

Great, guess he was going to fire me, and I hadn't even told him what was going on. Kody knew already, but I asked him to let me talk to his dad. We needed to work this out between us.

As he jumped down from the last sawhorse to the ground, I stood to wait. This man believed in me when

Thia Finn

I needed work and a place to live. I hated letting him down.

"So, boy, what'd they say?"

I looked around at Kody who walked toward us. He had told his dad where I'd been. Keeping secrets between father and son must be unheard of at this business.

"Well, Mr. Richards, I wanted to talk to you first, but I suppose Kody's already told you what's going on." I glanced at Kody who gave me a quick nod.

"Yeah, he did. I knew it was something because it's not like you to not come to work."

"Right," I stammered around trying to remember my rehearsed speech. "A man from a recording company came into the bar this past weekend and told me to come see him this week. I went in this morning to hear what he had to say." I stopped and looked Mr. Richards in the eye. "He had me play and sing for him, and the bottom line is, they want me."

Kody let out a loud whoop for everyone on the job site to hear. Sharing the news with the world wasn't my plan, but Kody thought differently.

"That's great, Becks. I'm happy for you to finally get to do what you came here for." Mr. Richards stuck out his hand for me to shake and pulled me in for a hug. His gesture surprised the hell out of me.

After hearing some well wishes from the guys, Mr. Richards started asking questions. "When does he want you?"

Becks

"He wants me in every evening this rest of this week to rehearse with a band on some of my songs." Explaining the rest of what Mr. Shandell wanted, Mr. Richards listened to it all.

"You've got music already written? How come we hadn't heard any of it yet?" he continued.

"Just hadn't had a chance to play for y'all." I never considered they would be interested in listening to me.

"Hell yeah, we want to hear ya play." Several of the guys standing around made similar comments. "Let's break for lunch, and he can give us a private concert. When's he's big and famous, we can say we heard him first at a construction sit outside Nashville, right guys?"

The group made a lot of noise with words and applause. My first private concert occurred in Harless, Tennessee, in front of ten framers, six roofers, three helpers, and an inspector that happened to be driving by. What a start.

NEWS REPORT FOUR

Anchor: From time to time, we like to check in on the progress being made to solve crimes in our area. Today we are taking a look at a fire that occurred in northeastern Lawback County. Our own Janna Alfred covered the residential fire and has returned to the scene to gather more information. Janna, what have you learned about this fire?

Reporter: We did learn that since the next of kin could not be located, a former worker for Judge Masters stepped in for the identification. At this point, the search for their two sons is still happening.

Anchor: Judge?

Reporter: Yes, it seems Beckon Masters was an influential county judge at one time. He apparently retired early from an unknown illness. His wife and two sons cared for him prior to the fire of the house.

Anchor: Janna, can you tell us any information about the home itself?

Reporter: (reading from notebook) Yes, Lisa. The wooden-structured home was built in 1910, making it vulnerable to any type of fire. Because it's located so far out in the county, there are no fire hydrants, so all water had to be brought in by tanker truck impeding the firemen from doing their jobs. Judge Masters was in his sixties, and Mrs. Masters was in her fifties. We were told the bodies were believed to be on the second floor of the structure which was built off the ground on blocks, as is common for this type of home. Also, there appeared to be a small apartment behind the home. The fire spread to the apartment before the firemen arrived, but they were able to save at least of a portion of that structure. From what we've learned, no bodies were found in it.

Anchor: Thank you, Janna. We'll continue following this story as more information is reported.

Chapter 5

SOPHIE

"Anything for you, doll." Mr. Chambers sat in the area of the club I covered for as long as I'd been here. Big tips weren't his thing but a smile always greeted me, and he patiently waited for his Jack and Coke. The old guy only allowed himself two drinks, then he'd say goodbye and head home to his wife.

I leaned back against the bar as he picked up his cap and left his two-dollar tip. He didn't need to tip me, and I'd told him many times. Just having a pleasant conversation with him and his wrinkled smile gave me all the pleasure I needed to serve him.

"You think his wife is alive?" Andi asked as she dumped the ice out of the used hi-ball glass.

I turned to her. "What makes you think she's not? He talks about her all the time."

Becks

"Yeah, I know he does, but have you ever seen her? Don't you think he might bring her in here once in a while?"

I placed my filled drink order on my tray. "I guess. Never really thought about it. Maybe I'll ask him next time."

"You mean tomorrow night?" She smiled at me. Andi's bartending was always fast and efficient which made for better tips for me.

As I delivered the drinks, two guys sat at a clean table in my area. I nodded at one letting him know I'd be right there. This guy was H.O.T. hot, movie star hot. Maybe he was here from L.A. for a job. I didn't recognize him, but my good looks radar pegged out at ten plus. I couldn't tell much about his hair because he had it pulled up in a bun on the back of his head, so it had to be long enough for that. The color looked a dark blond, almost brown. The stubble on his face looked purposely trimmed that way like a lot of singers wore.

What caught my attention, though, was his body. His t-shirt was tight across his chest, and the sleeves of his shirt stretched to keep the skin contained inside. A tattoo peeked out at me as I got closer to the table.

The man with him wasn't bad either, but my sight was set on hot guy one and refused to let go. Both of them sported dark tanned skin, so either they worked in the sun, or they hit up a tanning bed on a regular basis. Personally, I'd never liked the idea of being in a wannabe coffin for fear of cancer.

With my back to them, I sat my tray down and picked up a couple of glasses. I needed a chance to straighten my ponytail caught low on my neck. Messy hair wouldn't help make a good impression. I turned back to them and realized my movements captured their attention. So they caught me primping. No big deal. Women did it all the time on the job.

"What can I get y'all?" I tried to make it sound like it was part of my boring job taking their order, but I failed miserably. It came out more light and airy like I was anxious to speak to them.

The hot one looked at my name tag before he spoke. "Sophie, I'd like a Corona, dressed please."

"I'll take the same, Sophie."

I nodded and turned heading to the bar wondering why they both said my name. Most customers couldn't care less to know what to call me.

Andi watched me walk toward her. "What'd they do for you to have that look on your face?" Their beers came from the coldest part of the cooler before she sat them on my tray.

"Nothing really. They both made a point to call me by my name after looking at my name tag, though."

"Damn, girl, two guys looking that good, you should've told them your name, along with your address, phone number, and next of kin. You know, just in case they want to take you home and keep you there long enough for someone to come looking for you." Andi winked at me because I knew she kidded about something like that.

"Don't say that. It's not funny." But I smiled at her anyway.

"No, it's not funny. Fun, maybe." She wiggled her eyebrows. Andi was forever trying to find me a date. I didn't need a date. I needed a job and flirting with the customers might lead me to getting fired.

The two men watched as I walked toward them with their beverages. Damn, how did I get this lucky to have not one but two hot guys sitting in my section? It only made my sexy parts—that had been placed in solitary confinement for such a long time—push to get out.

Long hair wound into a thick bun on the back of his head caught my attention every time I looked in that direction. While they were both fiery hot, this one created lust inside me just watching his movements. His thick, sinewy forearms led up to well-defined biceps hidden behind the tight black sleeves stretched across the table. The stubble on his face made me wonder how it would feel to run my lips across his perfect face, the square jaw, the bridge of his nose. What about down his neck? Would it prickle? Could I bite my way down to his perfectly formed shoulders that begged to be used as anchors while he did dirty things to my body?

Whoa, Sophie. Take a beat, girl. You've got work to do.

Placing the bottles on the table, I started to put the ticket down. "No, Sophie here's my card. Run a tab, please. We're here to celebrate tonight, and I'm buying." This came from the other guy.

"Oh, that's great. What are we celebrating? Birthday, engagement, getting married soon?" Did I really ask that?

The royal blue eyes of the long-haired guy met mine. His unbending gaze focused on every feature of my face before he finally gave me an easy answer. "No, nothing like that."

"No, ma'am. What we have in our midst is the newly signed, next big thing on the music row." Without taking his eyes off me, the unhappiness of his friend spilling the news would be met with harsh words the moment I walked away.

"Well, congratulations, and I'm sure when you're ready, you'll be wanting to celebrate as much as your friend does." Glancing over at the happy guy, I winked at him to try and lighten the mood before gathering the credit card and heading back to the register.

Andi leaned into the bar to get closer to me, anxious to hear what our conversation had consisted of.

"Well, what'd they have to say? Did you leave your number on the ticket?"

Becks

Laughing, I shook my head no. "They're celebrating. At least one of them is anyway. The hot guy with the long hair has reason to celebrate, but he didn't seem thrilled his friend gave out the information."

"What's he celebrating then, unexpected rug rat on its way?"

"No, nothing like that. He got signed to a recording contract." I looked at her knowing she'd commiserate with my lack of that good luck. My dream of getting discovered dwindled each day. Maybe I was destined to always work in a bar serving drinks to tourists looking for a good time in a Nashville club.

"It'll happen one of these days, Sophie. It takes time. You have to pay your dues with shit jobs and late nights. At least you're playing weekends now."

As I nodded, I saw movement out of the corner of my eye knowing someone sat at another of my tables. "Yeah, you're right, but I'd hoped to be done with this by now." I moved toward the table ready to address the three obviously intoxicated men. The drunken look in their eyes told me what to expect before I took two steps in their direction.

"Hey. What can I get you?" The three were young and carding them would be necessary. Drunks complained louder than most about that kind of thing.

"Hey there, sweet cheeks. How about you? Can we buy you for a few hours?"

"Uh, no." Crude propositions were nothing new, but I knew better than to make a fuss or it would only get

Thia Finn

worse. When a smooth palm wrapped around the back of my thigh and slid up, I squeaked and jumped backward hitting the chair behind me. Standing quickly, I squared my shoulders ready for him this time.

"Whoa, there, honey bunch. I didn't mean to frighten you." The handsy man stood.

"Don't touch me, please." My stern voice should have told him I meant business, but he failed to recognize sternness and determination when he heard it. His big hand closed around my arm and pulled me up on my toes and close to his face. Andi didn't have time to bring her bat or call the bouncer to the scene before the two celebrating men suddenly appeared on each side of the man and me.

"Let her fucking go." Low words growled past long hair's lips.

"For what? We were about to get to know each other."

"No, you don't want to do that." The royal blue of his eyes widened with each word he spoke. "Take your fucking hands off her, or this shit isn't going to have a good ending."

"You and your pretty fucking man-bun don't know what you're getting into. I'll toss your dumb ass over that banister before you can blow your fucking rape whistle." He laughed as he looked at his two companions still sitting in their chairs expecting backup he wasn't going to be receiving.

Becks

Thankfully, our two, huge, club bouncers stepped up to the scene. "Problems here, Sophie?"

Andi spoke up as she aimed her baseball bat at the men. "These three need to go. They're drunk and causing trouble, especially him." Her bat found its way into his gut harder than necessary, and the big man doubled over. "Please escort them to the front door, guys."

With their meaty hands, they took the drunks by the biceps and shoved them toward the front door. Guilt by association caused the quiet ones to have to leave too.

I watched the men who came to my rescue without being asked, return to their seats like they rescued people every day. I owed them a thank you. Being in debt to someone was not my style. I'd taken care of myself for years, but I knew when to do the right thing.

Andi grabbed two more of the cold ones they drank and sat them on the bar. "Thanks. I'll pay for them out of tips."

"No, you won't. Consider it hazard pay for on-the-job injuries."

My head jerked up. "What? They didn't injure me."

"Looked like you could be bruised from the way he had you balancing on your tiptoes. Now go thank the two helpers." She left me standing there looking at her as she moved down the bar to more patrons.

Chapter 6

BECKS

Watching that scene unfold in front of Kody and me, I prepared for a bad ending. I wondered if she recognized us when she came to our table as the two who watched her catch the bus in the middle of the night. The answer was no because if she didn't call us out when we called her by name, she wouldn't do so now.

Obviously, the three who fell into the chairs came in three sheets to the wind which surprised me. The door people usually kept that kind out of this bar. Guess they found themselves too busy, especially for a weeknight, to stop the drunks from walking through the entrance.

Becks

A slender arm set a cold bottle down in front of me. "Here ya go, guys. I appreciate you helping me out with those asshats. Who goes into a bar drunk?"

I glanced up at her, and a beautiful smile spread across her face. She had naturally plump lips just right for kissing and running my tongue across. The bottom one begged to be sucked into my mouth before my tongue dove in for a taste. They formed a bow when she pursed them together as she continued looking at me.

Reaching out as she put Kody's beer down, I wrapped my fingers lightly around her delicate wrist and slightly tugged it toward me as I examined it for bruises.

"What are you doing?" She tried to jerk it back.

"Hang on. Just looking to see if the man-handling left a mark on you."

She stopped wrestling and allowed me to turn it over and have my fill of the milky white skin. This girl needed a trip to the beach, but the skin tone highlighted her hazel-colored eyes surrounded by feathers of darkened eyelashes. When I'd had my fill of touching the soft skin, I let it go. She didn't move away as quickly as I thought she might, given the tug-of-war we played to let me see.

"I'm fine, really. I've dealt with a lot worse." She pulled the tray up against her body trying to hide behind it, but the pink tinge in her cheeks spoke of embarrassment.

Kody jumped into our conversation. "No woman should have to put up with douchebags touching her unless she wants to be." He cut his eyes over to me. "Right, Becks?" His clever plot of putting my name out there worked.

"Becks, huh? That's an unusual name. Family name or something?"

"Yeah, unfortunately. It's part of my old man's name. He thought naming my brother and me after him would make us all close like a family should be. Too bad it didn't work." I smirked to myself. The last thing I wanted in life was to be anything like my father. The name Dad skipped over him like a rock on the water's surface. Only, in this case, the rock sunk to the bottom before making a single contact with it.

"That's too bad. I never knew my dad." She looked over the banister at the band playing on the lower floor.

"Is that right?" This conversation took a turn to areas I least expected them to go. Talking about Beckon Masters never happened. I refused to waste my breath on that son of a bitch.

"Okaaay." Sophie dragged the word out. "I just wanted to say thanks, but I have to get back to work."

"You're welcome, anytime," Kody said, and I nodded agreeing with him before she spun around and went back to the bar.

Becks

"Why didn't you ever mention you had a brother?" Kody spoke before she was barely out of hearing range.

"Why would I? Haven't heard from him since I left home."

"Is he still at home?"

I spun the glass bottle around in my hand with the cold condensation rolling down it and the water chilling my palms. *Konan.* That's a name I had serious doubts I'd ever say again in my life. "Thought we were supposed to be celebrating?"

"Right, we are." He tipped his long neck close to mine, and I met it, clinking the glass together.

"Then mentioning him is the last thing I want to do." I looked straight at him. "Ever again."

Kody nodded his head. He knew that topic of conversation was forever off limits between us. "We need to finish up anyway. The old man expects us there early in the morning since you took off today."

He made his way to bar to settle up with the two women running it. Sophie turned and looked over at me. The excitement I enjoyed from the good news went by the wayside with thinking of my family. They each had their own way of spoiling whatever happiness I found on my own. It seemed like they enjoyed ruining my happiness. To hell with them all.

I pushed back my chair rougher than I'd intended when I stood. It crashed to the floor before I could catch it. Glancing over to the bar, all three looked at me with different expressions. One had a grin, one looked annoyed, and the only one who mattered seemed scared. *Dammit, we needed to go home.*

A short time later, I laid my head back on the headrest as Kody maneuvered from the crowded parking lot to the street partially filled with tourists. "You want to tell me what that was all about?"

"No, I don't." I looked out my window into the neon lights glowing from all the bar windows. Every corner of downtown Nashville had a music venue on it. Men and women from all over the country, hell, maybe even the world, came to make it in this city. *Why did I think I could do it too?*

"Dude, why didn't you tell Sophie it was us who watched her catch the bus? She's going to think we're fucking weird for not mentioning it the first time we saw her."

"Won't happen because there won't be a next time."

"Sure there will. She gave me her number to give to you." He pulled a napkin from his pocket and laid it in the seat between us. "Said when you're in a better mood to give her a call."

As I pushed the button to roll the window down, I snatched up the napkin and threw it out the window. "Fucking problem solved."

"Shit man. If you didn't want to talk to her, I sure as hell would've."

"No. You're not talking to her either. Women are fucking trouble. Don't you know that by now?"

Becks

He sped up and headed out of town on the highway. "You're a dumbass. You know that?"

"Uh huh." I closed my eyes and let my mind wander. I knew it was a dick move to throw it out but calling her right now wasn't a good idea. Thinking of Kody calling her irritated me, so I lost the number. We both knew where she worked and could find her anytime we were ready. Hopefully, he wouldn't be ready any time soon.

It wasn't as though I didn't like women because I did. Right now, though, all I could think about was how her working in a bar reminded me of how my mom supported Konan and me while we moved around. As soon as she thought someone asked too many questions in one town, she packed us in that silver piece of shit and hauled us to another place. Sometimes she took us to another state.

The old bastard caught us when we went south to Florida and brought us back home. Not once did he apologize to her or to us for the beatings he gave us, or the way he made us do all the chores in the house. Said if we were old enough to live on the run, we were old enough to keep house, so he didn't need to bring in outside people.

He thought he fooled us, but hell no. We knew. If someone came in the house, they would figure it out in no time. After the second or third time he dragged us back, our mother started drinking. He didn't care what she did as long as she was in his bed waiting for him. We heard them over and over until her sounds ended. Sometimes he'd beat her if he didn't like the words she used. She'd shut up fast on those nights.

Konan learned to pour her whiskey, too. As soon as his arms and hands could open a bottle and pour from it, he brought it to her. She drank in the bathtub in the mornings and in the bed in the afternoon. She didn't dare pass out on the couch and be there when he got home. So the two of us took care of each other and we did what we could to take care of her.

Once, we talked her into sobering up enough to drive. He'd broken her jaw but refused to take her to the hospital. Moving her mouth to swallow caused a lot of pain, so she didn't drink for several days. We watched her shake some but at least she sobered up. After begging for hours, we talked her into leaving again.

We planned it for days because this time coming back wasn't an option as far as Konan and I were concerned. She drove us out of his mansion in the hills, as he liked to call it. We went west and then north taking highways and only stopping in big cities. When we got to Montana, we stayed in the car a few days and then found a motel to live in. She changed her last name back to O'Donnell.

Konan and I never figured out how she did it, but she got birth certificates with that as our last name too. She wanted us to get an education but covered her tracks by saying we had been homeschooled so they tested us and put us in the right grade. I learned to play the guitar that year. I even had a friend.

Kody pulled into the driveway, and I climbed into my bed falling asleep. I didn't want to have nightmares again. I hoped all this thinking I'd been doing didn't cause one.

Working all day and playing music half the night wore me out after the first week. When Saturday night rolled around, and I didn't have a gig, I decided to crash and burn until Monday morning on my pillow.

Mr. Shandell had other ideas because I stepped into the shower after his phone call and let the hot water roll down my sweat-soaked skin. Each day grew hotter as the summer approached and working in the sun made me more irritable. I needed to suck it up though because he wanted me to go down to an open mic night and play some of the music we'd been working on.

Getting my name around Nashville to widen my fan base needed to happen before we recorded the music. Live performances would show up on YouTube if people thought I was any good, and that would be a tremendous help when the first EP hit the market.

Social media and YouTube ruled the world now. I needed to be part of it all.

I'd not paid too much attention when I walked into the club. I signed up and carried my guitar case to the bar with me. I leaned over the bar as I climbed onto the stool and ordered a beer without noticing who sat on the next stool, but when the blonde curls swung around to show her face, I knew immediately.

"Becks, what are you doing here? Figured you'd be out on your first big tour by now." Sophie spoke loud enough for only me to hear.

"No, not yet. Been rehearsing with a band. The producer wants to lay some tracks before we bring it to any clubs."

She nodded as if she understood. "You know we weren't ever actually introduced, but since you never called, either your friend didn't bother to pass on my number, or you didn't want to talk to me."

"It's not like that at all." I put my hand out to her. "I'm Becks O'Donnell." She slid her soft hand in mine.

"Sophie Turner." We shook for a moment, and since I didn't want to let it go, I held on longer than necessary. This girl's beauty captured my attention both times I'd talked to her, but tonight she seemed even more stunning. Maybe it was because she hadn't been working a shift at the bar or maybe it's because I found myself attracted to her like no other woman I'd met. Her makeup looked perfect for performing, a little too heavy for my taste, but the stage tended to

Becks

need it that way. With her light coloring and eyes, I felt sure she needed it under the harsh stage lights. Some women used makeup like a shield, but from the subtle amount she wore, I doubted she used it as a defense.

"So, Sophie Turner. You cocktail waitress in a club to live and sing in a club to accomplish your dreams?"

"Strange way to look at it, but yes, you're right. That's exactly what I do."

"You want to be the next big female in country music?" With that comment, I got a huge laugh.

"No, no, no... I don't like most country music. I prefer to play alternative rock. At the club, though, they want me to only do cover songs. Have I said how much I hate that yet? My roommate says I repeat it all the time, like a mantra or something."

We both laughed, an easy way between us. As I listened to the melodious ring in her voice, I thought of my mom saying my time would come. That was before fire turned my life upside down. I shook my head to send that thought to the dark box in the back of my mind. No need to ruin my night with that old story.

"And what about you, what's going to make it on your first platinum album?"

"Too soon for that, I assure you."

"Too soon to tell about your music or about your first album going platinum? You should let me be the judge of that after we play."

The DJ called my name.

"Guess I'm up." I looked hard at her beautiful face. "And now my first critic waits to judge me. Be kind, please." A brief smile bowed my lips.

"Always." I slid off the stool and picked up my guitar case before nodding at her.

"Becks?"

"Yeah?"

"Break a leg, knock 'em dead. Oh, and take your hair down. It's too pretty to keep all tied up that way. The girls will like it better."

"Sure thing, Miss Turner. I aim to please the women." I winked at her and walked to the stage pulling the leather strip out of my hair.

Chapter 7

SOPHIE

Watching him walk away in tight, torn up, black jeans hugging his cute ass, I knew his performance would outshine mine. I should've volunteered to go before him like several others did. Tonight I wanted to sing one of my songs. The opportunity didn't happen often for an open mic night to play with my work schedule.

Becks moved confidently to stand behind the single mic in the middle of the small stage. He greeted the audience with a killer smile, complete with a pair of dimples, and then spoke as though he talked to old friends sitting in front of him. Having the ability to hold them in your hand before you sing a note must be nice. It was all I could do to say my name and sing the song. At home, I could sing and play my own songs like no other, but looking out across a sea of faces waiting to love or hate me, caused my stomach to churn.

I snuck a peek at the audience watching him. The look on the women's faces spoke of lust simply from the beauty of his own. If he captured them with his voice too, they'd all be eating out of the palm of his hand before the song ended.

Becks' fingers strummed across the strings, filling the room with a melodious sound, followed by the first chord before he launched into a riff proving his seemingly innate skills. The music surrounded the room capturing everyone's attention, and then he leaned into the mic and sang the words. His rich sound accompanied the notes, and the audience fell in love. He held them and me until the final note drifted away.

Loud applause, whistles, and shouts of praise blew up the room as he took a final bow and waved walking toward me.

"God. Now I have to wow them." I knew it sounded bitter before I finished the last word, and Becks heard each one.

"Come on, Sophie girl. Show 'em what you got. I'm sure you'll fair just as well as I did. They seem pretty friendly tonight."

"Yeah, some nights I want to throw bottles at them for being such assholes."

Becks

Becks laughed. "Then be glad tonight's not that shitty of a group. They even laughed at my stupid jokes."

"Yeah, but I don't look like a god on stage or have a single dumb joke for them."

He looked up at me from where he loaded his guitar case. "What? Have you looked into a mirror, Sophie?"

Becks stood and walked toward me. "You are oh, so mistaken. You're a beautiful woman. Why would you say such a thing?"

Looking down, I knew I wasn't ugly but beautiful could hardly be the right word. "I guess old habits die hard."

His warm hand cupped my cheek pulling my face up to look at him. "I don't know who said something like that to you, but they need to be smacked down. You're gorgeous and a hard worker and determined. You've planned for this night, and now I want you to shine for these people. Show 'em how it's done."

His soft lips kissed my opposite cheek, and our closeness allowed his scent to drift over me. He smelled like heaven, a woodsy cologne that set my senses reeling. He slid his hand off my cheek letting his thumb brush my skin. I wanted nothing more at that moment than to wrap my hands around his neck and pull him in for a kiss. A long, hot kiss. One that took my breath away and maybe left him panting.

"Here she is, ladies and gentlemen. Give a warm welcome to Sophie Turner who'll be performing one of her own songs tonight. Sophie," our host announced and held out his hand giving me the signal to move on stage.

"Go do it, woman. Do for yourself. Hell, do it for me." Becks gave me a little push to get me moving.

My shiny black shirt shimmied across my skin as I walked toward the mic. Even though sweat formed on my back and threatened to roll down my skin, I tried to look at ease as I turned and faced the crowd. Singing my own music was a huge risk since most of the time I faced an audience to sing someone else's songs.

With the strap wrapped over my shoulder, I strummed a few chords and took some deep breaths to calm down. I glanced back to see Becks looking at me from the small wings of the stage and nodding his head. This man, a total stranger really, saw something in me. He pulled for me even when I couldn't pull for myself. People, whose blinded faces kept them anonymous to me, began clapping trying to offer encouragement of their own to get me started.

The first chords to my music finally began, taking on a life of their own from memory. My consciousness slowly caught up with me, and I started to softly play the notes. Dammit, I needed to get my act together. I couldn't bomb out here and make a fool of myself like this.

Becks

A warm hand touched my back before I heard the same sequence of chords my memory strummed. I leaned into the mic.

"Hello, everyone. You'd think I was new to this when honestly, I've been playing most of my life." The soft notes continued behind me. "I want to play one of my own tonight, and I hope you enjoy it. This song is called "*The Last for You.*""

I continued playing with Becks standing a step behind me out of the spotlight. I was the one they saw. I was the one they heard. My confidence grew stronger with each note, so by the time I reached the second verse, I performed it the way it should be done, strong... confident.

My voice grew richer along with my playing, but that soft boost behind me stayed until my last note fell away on the breeze to a silent room.

Then, the audience clapped and yelled comments making me feel like a million bucks. I'd done it. My own music was out there now. Music written from my heart and my own hand received love by strangers.

I turned and held my hand out for them to acknowledge Becks, but the spot where he stood sat empty. He looked at me from the wings and smiled, allowing me to take all the credit for our performance. I took a deep breath and enjoyed the spotlight. *Could I love a man I didn't even know?*

Stepping off the stage and over to the bar, we knocked back a cold beer, and it helped soothe my throat from singing. I giggled at something Becks' friend, Kody, said. These two could keep me laughing all night the way they played off each other like a stand-up comedy act.

A man I didn't recognize walked up to us and stuck his hand out to Becks.

"Good job, Becks, and you too, Miss Turner. The audience loved you both." I nodded my appreciation having no idea who this man was.

"Thanks, Mr. Shandell." Becks spoke loud enough to make sure I caught his name.

"Please, call me Ethan." He turned to me. "I'm Ethan Shandell, Miss. Turner. My company is now representing Becks, but from what I saw here tonight, we probably should be repping you as well."

"Me?" I knew my voice sounded like a tortured bird. "You want to represent me?" I repeated myself. I couldn't believe what I was hearing. Turning to Becks, I raised my eyebrows, and his smile spread across his face.

"We signed Becks this past week, and we're always looking for raw, new talent. What I'd like to do is hear the two of you together. Can we make that happen on Monday?"

"Monday?" My parroting of everything he said sounded ridiculous, but I was seriously questioning my sanity over what I'd heard.

Shandell nodded. "What about that, Becks? She could come to your rehearsals with the band."

Becks

"Sure, sounds like a great idea to me, too." Becks also nodded at me.

"Well, I, uh..." My mind raced like a winner on Kentucky Derby day.

"Is there a problem with Monday?" Shandell asked.

"No, no problem at all. I'll be there." My words came out in a huge rush. I jumped off my barstool and stood looking up to look at Shandell. "I'd be honored to come to the studio and play with him."

Kody made a coughing sound in the background, and I realized what an awful choice of words I'd used. "I mean. I'd be happy to work him... work with him," I quickly added. "I'm going to shut up now. This hole I'm digging is getting too deep even for me."

The four of us laughed easing the situation. "Sophie and I'll be there on Monday at seven."

"Seven?" I whispered. I worked at seven. We couldn't do it later? Missing work caused problems for everyone. If I gave up my shift, I missed the tips. At $2.75 an hour not getting tips put a huge dent in my paycheck.

"We'll be there, Ethan." Becks took over the response for both of us.

"Great. I have to run. You know I'm always in a hurry." He pulled a business card from his breast pocket. "I look forward to hearing the two of you."

We both nodded and watched him walk away. "What the fuck, Sophie?" came out of Kody's mouth before the manager was twenty steps away. "When a company like 13 Recordings comes knocking, you gotta be ready and willing, little lady."

His comments surprised me because honestly, I thought Becks was going to be the one complaining about my questions. I turned to him and saw the grimace on his face.

"I'm sorry. What can I say? I have a job, remember? You know, the one that pays my bills."

Becks leaned close to me. "Sophie. Do you hear the line of shit spewing from your mouth? If you get signed with a label, you won't need a waitressing job that has you riding a bus home at two or three in the morning. You'll be able to have a car or maybe even a driver."

"What?"

"I said—"

"Stop. I know what you said. Back up. How do you know I ride a bus home at that time?"

"I'm talking about you making it in the music industry, and that's what you heard? Sophie..." he stood and got up almost nose to nose on with me, "... you'll have a contract. You'll have money in your pocket."

"Answer my question, Becks."

Before Becks could speak again, Kody stood beside him, so they were both leaning over looking at me. "He knows because we were the two in the truck who tried to give you a ride home in the middle of the night. We're the ones who sat and waited to make sure you got on the damn bus."

Kody's tone told me he was proud of their little accomplishment on making sure I was safe, but I replied with anything but gratefulness. "I never asked either of you to babysit me while I waited on that bus. All you succeeded in doing was making me more nervous."

This time Becks got ahead of Kody. "We worried you sitting on that bench would make you a target for some drunk or a group of them. Neither of us was willing to leave you there alone, Sophie. What you did or do is fucking foolish."

"What I do is none of your business. I've been taking care of myself for years now, and I don't need two country hick, red necks telling me how to live my life. It's my life, and I'll come and go as I please." By the time I reached the last word, it sounded so high and shrill dogs should have been howling. How dare they tell me what I should be doing. I turned on my heels and stomped away. The last thing I needed or wanted was not one but two men telling me how to live. Fuck them.

I picked up my guitar case and opened my phone. I'd go home and celebrate my performance without those two douche nozzles telling me what to do. Tonight I splurged and ordered an Uber. I'd arrive home in style for the first time, ever. I damn well deserved it, just this once.

Chapter 8

BECKS

Swinging around, I faced a smirking Kody. "What the hell was that?"

"Yeah, she was pissed, and all we were doing was trying to keep her safe. Crazy woman. Guess she likes to live dangerously." Kody shook his head before he sat back down to his half-finished beer.

"Should be an interesting meeting on Monday night, if she shows." Surely, she wouldn't ditch this chance.

"Oh, she'll show. She's not dumb."

"Sophie's anything but. She ranks up there as one of the most stubborn women, but dumb? No." I shook my head and thought about our scene before she walked on stage. Some sparks flashed between us when I had my hands on the soft skin of her cheeks. It was probably just an in-the-moment thing, but I knew I'd be revisiting it at some point.

When the last sip of beer drained from the bottom, we headed home. Kody made sure to go by the bus stop but the bench sat empty, either she rode on it already or found a ride. I offered a silent prayer someone she knew took her home. My life had enough to worry about, and there wasn't room for a crazy woman too.

Monday's job offered more of the same. While it came to me when I needed work, doing the same thing each day would never be my choice of careers. I checked my phone at least a dozen times as the afternoon dragged on.

"Got someplace you'd rather be today, Becks?"

"No, not today, but tonight I do."

"That right? Is she pretty?"

I smiled up at Mr. Richards. "My guitar is a beauty. We've got a date with band practice."

"Oh yeah? They gonna keep you around this time?" He grinned when he said it.

"I hope so since the recording company hired them to play with me." I threw a board up to him with my chest slightly puffed.

"Got a pretty woman coming tonight, too," Kody added as he walked around the back corner with a slight smile playing across his face.

His dad glanced down and watched him go by. "One walking and breathing? I'll be damned. I about decided the two of you might not be telling us everything about what goes on in that little house you share."

Kody threw up double middle fingers to his dad. "Old man, you know I like pussy better than anything in this world, except maybe whiskey. I like it pretty well, too."

"Yeah, and that's exactly why your dumbass hasn't found a pretty woman that'll stay around. When you decide one's better than drinking, I'll know you're in love."

"Shit, I ain't falling in love. That's just too much work. Right, Becks?"

I watched this play out between the two. My old man never talked to me that way. He rarely ever spoke a kind word to anyone much less to my brother and me. If I ever had a kid, I wanted to have this relationship with my child. Hell, I wanted to talk with my kid about everything. No shutting him or her out like we were, afraid to say any more than necessary before escaping the room, escaping him.

Becks

"Becks? You sleeping?"

"Oh, no. Just thinking." I threw up another board where Mr. R waited, watching down on me.

"That'll get you in a lot of trouble, son. You better leave the thinking to her."

"No, no... not about a girl."

"It's okay if you were thinking about a guy. No judging here. We're progressive like that. I'd love my kid no matter who he loved." Mr. Richards looked at Kody. I knew he spoke the truth from the look on his face. It took me by surprise, though. Most rednecks leaned toward a straight and narrow path.

"Go back to work, old man. You're embarrassing yourself."

"I don't give a shit." Mr. R turned to the crew working on the site. "Hey guys, did y'all know I love my son?"

"Oh hell. Now I'll never hear the end of this. This crew will be giving me shit for a month." Kody spoke so only I could hear him.

A strange feeling inside my chest bubbled up. Kody didn't know how lucky he was to have a dad who felt no shame in telling people how he felt about his own. Not too many men I knew growing up would have made an announcement like Mr. R. did. Kody should be proud of him.

Funny comments sounded from around the work area, along with whistles and hoots, but Mr. Richards didn't care. "Okay, now you bunch of damn slackers, get back to work. We've had our fun. This boy down here's got someplace important to be, and it might involve a woman. Get to it because Lord knows we don't want him to be late."

I shook my head. "Thanks, Mr. R. Appreciate you looking out for me." I laughed and went back to unloading the stack of wood needed to finish up today's work.

Walking into the rehearsal room, a couple of the guys were warming up on drums and the bass. I nodded to them as I set down my case and took out my guitar. Her marks spoke of usage, but her sound captured the ear of everyone. Our love affair had been going on for quite a while now since she held the place of my one and only guitar I'd ever bought on my own.

"Oh, hello, Becks." I turned to see Ethan shutting the door. He glanced around the room, and I knew he was expecting to see Sophie. "She's not here, yet."

"You think she's going to show?"

I raised my eyebrows because honestly, I had no clue. I pulled my hair back and tied it up in a knot. "If I had to say, it'd only be a guess because seems like that girl does what she wants."

He laughed out loud. "Has her own agenda, does she?"

Ethan's rhetorical question went unanswered as I strummed across the strings listening to the sound. I stepped on the tuner at my feet to perfect the tone while we spoke.

"I'm not sure it's an agenda, but she does things her own way, that's for damn sure."

"Good to know ahead of time. Having a feel for how my client's going to do things makes my life a lot easier."

"I can tell you there's nothing easy about Sophie if that's what you're thinking."

"So what you're saying is she's a typical musician?" He looked up from the papers he read and smiled at me. His words weren't meant to be offensive to me.

I understood how musicians acted most of the time. A lot carried their hearts on their sleeves, and any little thing could set some off into a meltdown. I'd seen it happen a few times, and the stories I'd heard or read about said their behavior sometimes held catastrophic consequences for bands.

The door popped open, and the other two guys laughed as they walked through it. When they saw Ethan standing there, they stopped.

"Oh, hey, Ethan," the keyboard player said.

"Hello, guys. Something going on I need to know about?" His voice rose upward at the end in question

Thia Finn

along with his eyebrows, something I'd noticed he did all the time.

The second guitarist stood with one hand on his hip and the other scratching the back of his head. "We passed a woman on the sidewalk with a guitar case talking to herself. She paced back and forth while she did it. It struck us both as kind of funny watching her."

"Did you ask her if she needed help?" Ethan questioned.

He wondered, just like I did if it was Sophie.

"We tried to. She didn't seem to hear what we were asking so David touched her on the shoulder to get her attention. That crazy woman screamed like he tried to assault her. We both got the hell out of there and came inside."

Ethan looked at me. I nodded my head because we both knew the answer as to who it was. Before we could make a move, the door burst open slamming back against the wall.

"Oh, sorry." Sophie grabbed for it, but it was too late. "Uh... I mean, sorry I'm late." She caught the door before it bounced back around to bang against her. "I had to take the bus here right after they let me leave work, and I didn't get a chance to clean up or change or anything, so I'm here looking like a cocktail waitress, and I know that's not what you'd expect to see rehearsing, and I wanted to—"

"Stop talking, Sophie." I stood directly in front of her and lifted my hand prepared to place it over her

Becks

lips to keep her from spewing any more words all at once. "It's okay. We haven't started yet."

The two men who walked in last started laughing again. "Woman, do you talk that much all the time?"

Before she could rip them a new one, I wrapped my hand around her face, making sure to keep her lips trapped from whatever she planned to say. It wasn't going to be pretty. She reached up and pulled on my index finger talking the whole time behind my palm.

Ethan glanced at the four men watching the event unfold. "Why don't y'all take a short break and let me have a minute with these two? Preferably in the lounge and not here."

To keep Sophie contained, I had to wrap my arm around her waist because she immediately tried to back away from me and my silencing palm. When the guys shut the door behind them, I looked at her closely. "You gonna hit me when I let you go?"

The look I saw in her eyes told me she might. She finally stopped resisting and nodded. The space between us held electricity that sparked from both sides. Hers came from anger, and I didn't want to even think about where mine was coming from.

"Okay, I'm going to let you go now. You good with that?" She glared at me but nodded again.

Ethan stood beside me as I released her completely and took a short step back.

"What the hell, Becks? Why would you keep me from speaking?"

Page | 89

"I thought you might say something you would live to regret from the look on your face." It took everything in me to not smile as I said it. Damn, she looked so cute all riled up that way.

Sophie stopped and pulled in a deep breath. I prayed she used the time to think before she spoke. The last thing Ethan wanted to work with was someone who couldn't control themselves over such minor things. Getting laughed at by your co-workers was nothing if we all went on the road together. Sophie needed to show him she could be a team player, not a diva.

She turned and looked at Ethan. "Sorry. I don't usually get upset that easily, especially when I knew they were joking. It's been one of those days, you know?"

He patted her on the shoulder. "We all have those days, Sophie. Don't worry about it. Did you have problems getting here?"

"No, not once I got off. We had it scheduled so I could be off an hour early, and my relief didn't show. My manager had to scramble to find someone else, or I wouldn't be here at all."

"We're glad someone did then, and you're here now. It's all going to work out fine, and please don't think anything about the two who laughed. Those guys were just busting your b... well, anyway, they like joking around."

Becks

"Good. I'll remember that when paybacks roll around. You know, karma and all. I can joke, too." A sweet sound that made my heart feel good passed over her pretty heart-shaped lips. All the times I saw her so far were connected to something stressful. It made me happy to know she had a lighter side.

Chapter 9

SOPHIE

"Before the others get back in here, Sophie," Ethan began. "I wanted to talk to you about the bout of stage fright you experienced at the club."

I hoped he had forgotten about that little scene, so we could move on but apparently not. "Yeah, I'm sorry you had to see that. Sometimes I psych myself up too much, and it causes anxiety, you know?"

"Then it's happened to you before?" Ethan's concern highlighted his face.

"Just a few times." Admitting this could come back to haunt me, but I didn't want to skirt around the truth.

"Do you know what triggers it?"

"That night, when I followed Becks, a little doubt crept in. The longer he played, the more nervous I

Becks

got." I hated saying this in front of Becks, but since he'd rescued me, I decided to tell the truth.

"Me? I caused your anxiety? No way." Becks' sapphire eyes drilled me.

"I stood backstage listening and watching the audience respond to you. All I could think was damn, if they love him, they'll hate me. My first instinct was to run." I stopped and turned to Ethan. "Of course, I didn't, but I wanted to."

They had no way of knowing that running was always my first instinct. I tried to avoid conflict, but somehow I usually found myself in the middle of it.

"We're glad you didn't, Sophie. Aren't we, Becks?" Ethan nodded in Becks' direction.

"Hell yeah, we are. You did a great job that night, but you gotta figure out how to pump yourself up before you walk on stage. If listening to someone else is going to cause you problems, then pop in your earbuds and cut out their sound. Simple as that." Becks' eyes fixed on me as though I should've discovered this solution on my own.

"Since it doesn't happen all that often, it never crossed my mind to try something to prevent it."

Becks grinned. "So what you're saying is, it was me who caused the problem for you?"

"Don't let that ego float you above the rest of us, Becks. It's happened with a few other performers, too," I added. He continued to keep the pleased look on his face.

"Yeah, yeah. I know what you're saying. You just have a thing for my music, or is it my good looks that do it for you?"

If my eyes could roll any higher in my head, I'd be blinded. "Keep thinking that, big boy." Looking over at Ethan, I added, "You think his head has grown large enough for us to work around? He might need to be onstage alone, so there's room."

"Ha, ha." Becks' comeback didn't sound so amusing then.

"Now that the stage fright mystery has been alieved, let's talk about you two playing together. You always play solo, Sophie?"

"Yes. I've never had anyone offer to work with me." Thinking about performing with another person on stage made me wonder how it would be. How would it sound? When Becks chimed in to get me straight on the stage, we made a good team. He easily picked up on the music. I could work with him.

"What about you Becks? You ever share the stage with anyone?"

Becks stopped strumming and glanced at me and then looked at Ethan. "Yeah, but it's been forever, like another lifetime ago." From the look he hit me with, I felt like there was more to his answer than he wanted to share.

The musicians opened the door and trickled back in, moving behind their instruments. Ethan dropped his line of questioning. Maybe he decided to wait, or

Becks

maybe he didn't need me if Becks wasn't willing. We didn't talk contract as he'd done with Becks. He invited me to sit in with them, that's all.

Ethan finally spoke up. "So here's what I would like to see today. I know everyone but Sophie practiced a few days last week on Becks' songs. I would like to see how her voice can add to the overall sound."

He turned to me. "Sophie, you won't need to play your guitar for this. You concentrate on accompanying Becks on the words." He pulled sheet music from a binder and handed it to me. "Why don't you listen to them play it through once, and then we'll add you to the mix?"

Looking at the music, I could play the song, but with two guitars already filling out the sound, it wasn't necessary. When they added a bass and a keyboard to it, a full sound richly accompanied Becks' voice.

I loved the soulful song. He caused the little hairs on my arms to stand as he sang the last word. The beauty of what he wanted to say came across with all the chosen words. Becks truly knew what he was doing when it came to writing music.

Watching him lean into the mic and sing the lyrics changed the way I saw him. This man held me in the palm of his hand until the last note just like he did an audience. If I hadn't been so nervous at the club, he would have captured me that night. He could do a private performance for me, and I'd die a happy woman.

My idolizing reverence jerked to a halt when I realized Ethan called my name.

"What?"

"I said, 'what'd you think?'" He knew I loved it already. I could see it in the look he gave me. Did this guy live to feed Becks' ego? They hadn't even known each other all that long, had they?

"Y... yes. I loved it. Everything about it... the words, the music, the sound, the band behind him. It was all great."

"Do you want to try it with him this time?"

"Me? What could I possibly add to that? The song was perfection." I looked at Becks who smiled at me. Not a smirk or a grin but a genuine smile, as though he appreciated what I said.

"Yes, it was great, but I want to see how the two of you sound together. We probably won't have you both singing on every song, but I thought this might be a good one to try out."

I slowly turned back to Becks. "What do you think?"

"Hell, yeah. Let's do it." He looked at the band, and they all nodded.

Taking my place behind the mic, things seemed weird without my guitar. Maybe it provided me comfort of not being alone in front of a sea of unknown faces. I looked around at the band and at

Becks

Becks. Having them here with me, I would never be alone.

Becks watched me as I wrapped my hands around the mic stand. We nodded at each other, and he looked back at the band just before the drummer counted off the beat. As Becks began singing, I harmonized with him through the entire thing.

The more we sang, the more I realized this didn't need me singing every word. This required me filling in, backing him up.

When we finished, I jumped up and down with excitement. My thoughts and adrenaline were pumping. "Let's do it again. I want to do it differently this time."

Becks raised his eyebrows. "Oh, yeah?"

"Yeah. I have another idea."

"You heard the lady, guys."

The drummer once again tapped his sticks together. Ethan looked at us through the glass of the control room. All of the sliding controls of the engineer sat in front of him. He put on a pair of headphones to listen to us, and the longer we sang, the more his face shifted from concerned to pleased.

This time when the last note from the guitars faded out, we all smiled. We'd successfully changed the way it sounded. While I thought it was perfection before, now we all knew it had what it needed with my voice sometimes accompanying him and sometimes backing him up.

Thia Finn

The speaker crackled on, and Ethan's voice spoke to us. "Let's do that once more, and I'm going to record this time. I want you to be able to listen to it."

We all nodded and started again. Each time we did the song, it improved even if it was ever so slightly. The rehearsal went on longer than I dreamed it would.

Ethan called us into the booth a few times to hear the recordings. He seemed pleased with what he heard. Finally, he turned the sound on in the rehearsal room.

"Sit down and listen to this," he told us. "I think you're both going to be happy with what we've changed since the first rehearsal. I know I am."

The song started with the familiar drummer's clicks. What we heard over the speaker seemed like a completely new song from what we started the night with. Our voices melded together as though they were meant to be one. I kept thinking over and over, this is beautiful. This is what it was meant to be. Our other halves had been found. From union to team. And now, a flawless duo.

We listened a few more times until I yawned and looked up at the huge clock above the window. "Oh, wow."

"Yeah, it's getting late, and I have work tomorrow." Becks headed toward his case and began putting away his guitar and music.

Becks

"Me, too." I picked up the phone and realized the buses were not running by my house still. I'd have to wait for an Uber. Not too many hovered late in this area of the city. "Shit."

"What's wrong?" Becks walked back to me.

"Oh, nothing." He watched as I pulled up the app on my phone.

"Don't do that. I can drop you off."

"No, it's fine. I take them all the time." This wasn't exactly a lie. I did use them sometimes. Rarely, but sometimes. Well, maybe once every six months...

"It's not too fine with me. I mean, I know they vet drivers now, but it's money out of your pocket to take it when I'm in my truck already. Who knows how damn long you'll have to wait for them to get over from Broadway. That's where they hang out this time of night. Those crazy-ass drunks needing a ride home and all."

The truth in what he said caused me to think harder about getting a ride with him. Depending on others bothered me. I would owe him if I did.

"Can I pay you? I mean, I'd pay an Uber, why don't I pay you instead?" He cocked his head to one side and scrunched his eyebrows together. I swear, this guy used every muscle in his face to talk for him.

"Yeah, uh, no. You can't pay me. I don't have an Uber app or a license to take money from riders, so I won't be collecting any money in my PayPal account tonight."

"But you don't understand. If I don't pay you, then I'll owe you, and I don't like owing people when I can pay. I'd feel better about it all if you'd let me pay and—"

He put a finger to my lips to shut me up. "Stop, right there. You get carried away too easily, Sophie girl."

With my hand wrapped around his thick forearm, I pulled his finger from my lips but not before he took the time to slowly brush it back and forth completely across them. He did it as though he enjoyed the feeling of the softness or maybe it was the plumpness. My bottom lip became slightly swollen from all the times I'd sucked it in and bit it while concentrating on the music.

When he did this, two things happened. First, I looked at his forearm where his shirt sleeve had been rolled to. The muscles were thick and well defined which made me wonder what he did to keep them looking that way. Second, his fingers moving over my lips sent some juju down me that lit up all the wrong parts. I felt on fire down the core of my body.

My nipples perked to tight points, and I prayed my bra kept them from showing, but I couldn't concentrate on that because I buzzed between my legs like a vibrator laid inside me turned on high. Damn. It had been a long time, but not so long that having a man touch my lips would send me straight to a lustful haze.

Becks

His eyes turned to a darker color as he watched me. Letting go of his arm, I took a step back from him. "Okay, I accept your offer. You can drop me off. Thank you." Before he could say a word, I made a dash for my guitar case and closed it being careful to snap the locks with a loud click.

No, no, no. This can't happen. I'd worked too hard to get this chance, and nothing would stand between me and being successful in the music industry. And certainly not a pretty face like Becks'.

NEWS REPORT FIVE

Anchor: And now to update you on the fire that occurred in the northeastern part of the county. Janna, we understand some information about the bodies has finally been made public.

Reporter: The bodies have been identified, and the names have been made public after we filed a motion to obtain the information. The county has been very tight-lipped about handing out what should be public.

Anchor: Why do you feel like this information was suppressed?

Reporter: Good question. All we've been able to find out is the two people who lived there are indeed the two bodies found. They are identified by dental records as Beckon and Laura Masters. As you may know, Beckon Masters is a former judge in that area so many knew him and his wife. They were considered prominent citizens in the area.

Anchor: We're sorry to hear this. I'm sure they will be missed. What about the next of kin. Did they have children?

Reporter: Yes, two sons, who are adults and apparently don't live in the area any longer.

Anchor: Thank you, Janna. I'm sure you'll be keeping us posted as the story unfolds.

Chapter 10

BECKS

The speedometer rose with my old truck pointed to the edge of Nashville. The gauge's light and the occasional streetlamp provided a glow between us. The last thing I expected when I headed into Nashville tonight was having a beautiful woman riding in the other bucket seat on the way home.

Sophie sat as close to the door as she could possibly squeeze. It made me wonder if she thought I planned to attack her or something. What I was most afraid of was her changing her mind and jumping out the door at any moment. Her body language read 'ready to bail at the first opportunity.'

"If you gave me your address, I could put it in the GPS." I glanced at her.

Becks

"That's okay. It's not too much further. Turn left at the next light." She looked over and tried to form a smile on those gorgeous lips. Touching them made me want to kiss them. I spent the entire time we rehearsed watching her worry that lower lip between her teeth. The action had to be a habit because she did it every time something confused her or she needed to concentrate. I settled with running my finger over them. The softness held everything I'd been dreaming about too.

After I turned, she sat up as much as the seat belt allowed on the front of the seat. "What street do you live on?" Getting information out of her about her home was harder than restringing my guitar.

"This one. It's right up there. Those apartments on the left." Sophie pointed just ahead.

"Got it. I'll turn in to get off this street."

"Oh, no, that's fine. You don't have to." The brief looks I could make out told me she grew more anxious with each turn of my wheels.

"I have to go back the other way, so I might as well."

She took a deep breath and leaned back letting it out. "I live in a dump, but I guess you already knew that when you started toward this side of town."

"I lived in plenty of dumps when I was young. My mom moved us around often enough to outrun the disconnect notices and other bills she never intended to pay." Sophie needed to understand where I came from. I might have had money later in my life, but no silver spoon ever graced these lips. More like plastic we swiped from the corner store when we had enough to buy a few groceries.

A squeak from my breaks announced our arrival. "Sounds like you need to do a brake job on this old thing." She looked over and smiled, and I laughed out loud.

"That's the sexiest thing I've heard a woman say in ages."

"You get off on women who can do their own repairs, huh?"

"Sophie girl, you can talk mechanics to me any time you feel like it. Those words make me all kinds of riled up." We shared a laugh this time.

She rolled her eyes. "Men, you're so easy."

"Hey, I'm far from easy. I like to work for what I get."

"Good. I've worked for everything I've ever had."

"I'm not sure we're still talking about the same thing."

"No, I'm sure we're not because like every other guy I've ever been around, your mind went straight to sex."

"You're the one that said 'getting off.'"

"And you're fourteen-year-old self couldn't help it, right?"

"Damn right."

Becks

The tension I felt before melted with our light-hearted conversation. Maybe she needed a chance to get to know me some before she felt comfortable.

"Guess, I'll get out now." She gathered her bag and opened the door. I knew I should have walked around and opened it for her, but I was afraid she would see it for something more than we needed. Seeing her guitar case on the back seat, I decided it was enough of an excuse to get out, though.

I opened the door, grabbing the handle on the case as she rounded to meet me at the front of the truck for the handoff.

"Thanks a lot, Becks, for giving me a ride. I promise I won't make a habit of it."

"It's actually on my way home. Kody and I live out in Commerce. It's about twenty miles out of Nashville in this direction."

"Yeah, I've heard of it. I assumed you lived in town."

An awkward silence fell between us until I held up the case. "Oh, yeah. Here ya go."

"Well, thanks again, Becks. I'll see you tomorrow night, right?"

"Sure thing. We've got a lot more songs to work on."

She leaned against the front bumper. "About that. Where do you see this going? I mean, I haven't been offered a contract like you have." She glanced down at her phone and saw the time. "Oh, never mind. It's late.

We can talk about it tomorrow night on a break or something."

"No, it's a legit question, but you need to talk to Ethan privately about the numbers end of it. I'm only the musician."

She stood and took a few steps up the sidewalk toward a dark doorway. "See you tomorrow."

"Yeah, goodnight." I watched as her steps sped up getting to the door and putting her key in it. No way would I leave her standing out here alone. "You should leave a light on tomorrow night." I spoke loud enough for her to hear me as she turned the knob, and the door opened. She flipped on the porch light.

"Will do, Dad." The laughter in her voice told me she had no fear, but I felt better about her entering the dark cavern. If she was happy living here, who was I to question it.

Holding a real conversation with her even though it wasn't about anything important gave me a better feeling about working with Sophie. She seemed so stressed, and in a hurry every time we'd met. Talking gave me a chance to see the real woman under all the weight she seemed to constantly carry on her shoulders.

The drive home went quickly with my mind on her. Rehearsal went better than I expected. I hoped it seemed that way to the others listening. Ethan's opinion of her, of us, meant a lot toward our success.

Becks

If she impressed him tonight, then her chances of her getting signed would improve.

Sophie learned the few songs quickly, both the lyrics and the music. That made her more valuable to all of us. We wouldn't have to wait around for her to catch up. Ethan made it sound like he wanted us out performing as quickly as we got it all together. I was down with that. I hoped she saw it that way too.

Darkened windows lined the front of our house when I drove in the driveway. I opened the door only to hear Kody's loud snoring shaking the rafters. Good thing I wasn't there to rob him. The guy could sleep through a tornado.

A dim light shined over the kitchen counter, and a piece of mail lay unopened on it. My name peeked at me through the clear window. Since I rarely ever received mail, ignoring it wasn't an option. I unfolded an entire page of information waiting to be read.

Scanning down the page, I reached for the envelope to read the return address. If I'd done that first, I might've been more hesitant to open it. Bold blue letters in the corner read Lawback County Sheriff.

My past needed to stay in Lawback County.

The thick paper crumpled in my hand as I opened the garbage can lid and dropped it in.

My t-shirt landed on the floor next to my jeans as I crawled in my unmade bed. Everything about me was tired. I'd worked a long day at the job, but the time we spent practicing took more out of me but in a good

Page | 109

way. I loved playing music and adding Sophie to the mix amped up my need to work harder.

I rolled over and stared at the pattern on the ceiling caused by the streetlight. My brain was spent so why couldn't I turn it off? *Sophie.* Adding another voice, another musician, another sound to my songs had never been an issue before. *Would having her with me be an issue now?*

If we had a chance to travel, what kind of problems would her being around cause? Putting a female in with a bunch of men might create all types of situations. She didn't seem like the kind to depend on anyone else, so I figured she was self-sufficient but being the only woman, I just didn't know.

What I did know was I found myself attracted to her already. How would that go over living in close quarters on a bus or traveling? Distractions weren't a good thing when I needed to stay focused on my music. She was too beautiful not to be noticed. Hell, I'd already gone out of my way noticing her. As I closed my eyes, all I saw was her soft lips that my fingers made the mistake of touching. I groaned and rolled over.

Chapter 11

SOPHIE

Sandpaper. Ugh. The scratching my eyelids did when I opened my eyes for the first time was at a whole new pain level than I'd felt in ages and damn, I wasn't even hung over. Not that I did that much drinking because when I did, my eyes usually ending up feeling this way. At least my head didn't have that pounding going on like a hangover always caused me.

I rolled on my side glancing at my phone. Once in a while I slept without an alarm and today was one of them. Technically, it was my day off but with rehearsals, I didn't know when I would get another of those.

So far my life held in a holding pattern waiting for a break to happen. I prayed this opportunity was what I'd been dreaming of.

Opening my phone, I found a text from Mr. Shandell.

"Oh boy, oh boy, oh boy." My feet hit the floor. I read it once and then again to make sure. He wanted me to come an hour before rehearsal so we could go over my contract.

"My contract." I had a contract. *"A contract."*

As I danced around in my efficiency apartment, I bumped into everything, but it didn't matter. My excitement was too much to contain. "Who can I call?"

My contact list didn't have too many numbers in it, but I knew Andi would be excited for me. The clock read only ten. "Too early to call her, she's still sleeping."

Scrolling through the numbers, my thumb stopped on my mom's. It'd been a while since we talked. She didn't support my choices in life and told me every chance she had. Her philosophy of going to college, find a husband, marry and have kids didn't fit so well with me. It wasn't the seventies anymore.

Mother, or Annie as she now insisted I call her, had me in the midst of her planned life, and it caused a kink in it. She still did everything on her agenda but only after pawning me off on grandparents who were too old to raise a child. Our relationship was never easy. She did what she wanted, and if I fit into that, then I was welcome. It rarely ever happened, though, so two elderly people did the best they could with a rambunctious child, pesky preadolescent, and a terrifying teenager.

I opened my text messages sending her one telling of my new adventure. If a reply came back, I'd be shocked since my accomplishments had little impact on her. Now that I was an adult, what she did worked the same way with me. We went our separate ways when I turned twenty. I'd spent most of my community college days caring for them, but when my grandfather passed, Annie showed up long enough to move Grammie into a home and basically told me to get a life.

Songwriting came naturally to me after I learned to play my guitar. I'd asked for one for Christmas and Annie sprung for a nice one, a Gibson CJ 165. She later told me that it's just like the one Miley Cyrus used in the Hannah Montana movie, which made me laugh. She said she figured if Miley Cyrus could play one, then surely I could. I didn't know whether to be insulted or flattered, but I knew it'd cost a lot of money, so I thanked her. My mother would never settle for something cheap, even for me.

I walked out the front door of the house I was raised in with a duffle bag of clothes and shoes and my guitar. The For Sale sign already had a SOLD sticker plastered across it, so I knew I was on my own. Nashville seemed like the best place to start if I planned to be a musician. Me and a thousand others had the same idea.

Luckily, Annie invested some seed money, as she called it. It allowed me to rent my tiny apartment, buy a few groceries and live for a couple of months. The stars must have been lined up for me that month because I found a cocktail waitressing job quickly. I watched my money carefully so the seed money would last as long as possible, and my job would take care of the rest.

After downing a few cups of coffee, I could finally focus my eyes. I liked to spend my rare off days doing as little as possible. It gave me time to recharge and prepare myself to do battle for the next six days.

Now I had something more important to do. Before leaving the studio last night, I grabbed copies of the sheet music to Becks' songs. If I could go in familiar with them, they might allow me to play along with them tonight. With my guitar in my hands, it felt more natural being behind a mic. All I could do last night was wrap my hands around the stand. If I didn't hold on to something as we sang, I felt like I might fly away.

The first time to have a full band behind me as I sang gave me so much to remember. The cues to come in on, the sound the keyboard added since it played around the melody as my backup singing did, and not stepping on Beck's voice all had to be accounted for. It took a few tries before I did it perfectly, and then sometimes I still messed up on something.

I practiced the songs we played the night before, making sure I had them down until I heard my phone

Becks

buzz. Guess she finally decided to treat me with an answer, even if it took her all day to do so. No such luck. The unknown number appeared but no caller ID. Usually, I let those go to voicemail, but it worried me that Ethan might be calling from a landline at the studio.

"Hello."

"Hey, uh… this is Becks."

"Becks?"

"Yeah."

"Oh, how'd you get my number?"

"I hope it's okay. I called, and Ethan gave it to me."

"Yeah, no problem. We should have each other's numbers." I'd add him to my contacts after the call.

"Hey listen, I thought we might meet up before the band arrived today if you're available. We could run through the songs to get you caught up."

"That's a great idea. I mean, if you have time to work with me. You're busy, so I completely understand if you don't."

"Sophie, I called because I want to rehearse together."

"Oh, right." Again, he wanted to help me. *Why did I question all of his offers of kindness?*

"I'd love to run through the music with you. Uh, actually, I sorta took sheet music to a lot of the songs last night, so I could work on them on my own before practice."

"That's great. Let's add me to the mix, and we'll both be ready to work this evening with the whole band."

"Right." Rehearsing with Becks before the band showed would be perfect. "I'll see you at the studio in an hour then?"

"Yeah, that's cool. You want me to pick you up on the way in? It's on my way, remember?"

"No, no. That's okay." *Think Sophie.* "I uh... I have something to do before you get there, so I'll meet you in the practice room." Lying didn't come easily to me, but I didn't want him to feel obligated to provide me with rides. I needed to meet with Ethan so I could take care of that as soon as I arrived.

"If you're sure. I don't mind."

"Thank you. Really. I appreciate the offer but like I said, I have something to do first. I'm leaving now, as a matter of fact." *Sort of a lie too.*

"Okay, I guess I'll see you in an hour or so." He didn't sound angry which eased my mind.

"Right. I'll see you then."

"Later." He ended the call before I could say goodbye.

Now, what to wear. Not like I had an extensive wardrobe, but it was only rehearsals. I dug through my closet and pulled out a Cold War Kids concert shirt. I found it at a great resale shop. I loved its soft feel and faded color. It would look perfect with torn jeans and my chucks.

Becks

The Uber driver's motor revved up in front of my apartment as I locked my door. *Impatient much?*

I opened the door and put my guitar in first. I refused to show up at rehearsals without it even if Ethan said don't bother.

"Ready?" His gruff smoker's voice asked.

"Sure." I barely had time to shut the door before he shot off from the curb. Thankfully, he didn't ask questions like the few I'd taken before had done. I eased open my case and pulled out the sheet music. I knew the words but I wanted to study the music.

Why waste time watching the back streets of Nashville fly by?

BECKS

"Come on. I don't have time for this." As I sat in traffic, I thought about Sophie. See the girl, meet the girl, make music with the girl. Hell, I might even be touring with the girl. Who knew at this point? She could sing, I'd give her that. The fact she was beautiful made her perfect for the stage. Fans flocked to talented people, and her looks would draw even more.

A Porsche slipped in cutting me off, and I slammed on my brakes. My fist hit the horn. Rush hour traffic in Nashville could be a nightmare. I needed to get my mind off her but dismissing those green eyes posed a whole new problem.

I rolled into the parking lot on time. Not too many people around in the early evening if the lack of cars were any indication. Office workers had taken off for the day, and the musicians always rolled in at the last minute.

Laughter rang out as I walked in the side door. The genuine sound said whoever it came from felt at ease to enjoy the moment. The noise made me smile to myself. Working in a positive atmosphere relaxed me. I never wanted to play music and feel like it was a job, but if drama and arguments existed, that's what it turned into. My life before coming here had enough problems for a lifetime, so the last thing I wanted was to be forced into that situation.

As I rounded the corner, the door to Ethan's office stood open, and Sophie sat across the desk from him. The smile spread across her gorgeous face told me the light-hearted sound came from the two of them. She said she needed to do something but failed to mention it was at 13 Recordings. It made me happy to know she relaxed sometimes.

I cleared my throat. "Hello."

Ethan stood. "Oh, hey, Becks. We were just talking about some of the dives Sophie's played here around Nash." He didn't owe me an explanation which made me wonder why he gave one.

"If it caused her to laugh that loud, those places must have been horror stories."

Sophie glanced up at me. "You don't even know. I've played some places I didn't really want my shoes to touch the floor for fear they would stick permanently."

"Sophie, why would you do that to yourself?" Why she would subject herself to places that bad?

"Well..." she looked away as though she rethought about her reply, "... I guess because I needed to know if anyone would want to listen to me. What if I sucked or couldn't carry a tune?"

My lips lifted in a slight smile. "That's what family and friends are for."

"No way. My grandparents would lie about it, and I was too afraid to play for friends."

"That's why they're friends. You can subject them to howling, and they should be okay with it."

"Yeah, but they might laugh at me, and adolescent me might not have survived."

Ethan joined in. "That's true. The Wicked Witch doesn't hold a candle to teenage girls these days. They'll say or do anything if what my youngest sister tells me is true."

"Believe me..." Sophie spoke softly, "... they can be snakes in the grass you don't see coming until the fangs are in your skin."

I watched her as she spoke. Obviously, she had been the recipient of this special brand of cruelty at some point in her younger life. Her face tinged slightly red, and her eyes spoke of a memory she preferred to forget. Sophie's face and eyes spoke volumes. The more time I spent with her, the more I realized how expressive they both were. I hoped I learned to read these expressions even better while we were

Becks

together. Anticipating her needs ahead of time could mean a lot on stage. Hell, I wanted to anticipate the off stage too.

"That's too bad because if they could hear you now, they would know you're an up-and-coming artist they should've listened to," Ethan praised.

"Right." Her reply held a cynical note which he obviously picked up on from his facial reaction.

"Anyway, Becks, I have some great news." She jumped up and grabbed a stack of papers off Ethan's desk.

"Yeah, what's that?"

She held up a contract. "I'm officially a new musician for 13 Recordings."

I stepped in and wrapped my arms around her lifting Sophie from the floor twisting her back and forth. "That's awesome, Sophie girl. Just awesome."

I held her longer than I should. I probably shouldn't have picked her up, but in the moment, it seemed like the natural thing to do. I wouldn't apologize for innocent praise.

When she pushed back a little and looked at me, I sat her back on her feet.

"Uh, sorry. I guess I'm happy for you."

She started jumping up and down. "Happy? I'm ecstatic. I've been dreaming about this moment for a long time."

Ethan laughed reminding us he was in the room. "Oh, let me think about this. You're twenty-four years old so by 'so long' you're talking ten years max?"

Sophie looked at him through her lashes trying her best to appear embarrassed. "Yeah, maybe. Besides, when you're young, everything you wait for takes forever, right?"

"True, but the waiting is over."

She stuck her hand out to Ethan. "Thank you, Ethan. Thank you for believing in me and trusting me enough to give me a chance. I do appreciate it, and I won't let you or 13 Recordings down. Ever."

"Well, Sophie, that's a tall promise. Ever... is a long time." Ethan shook her hand and let go.

"I know, but I do mean it. I don't ever want to forget this day. The day someone believed in me enough to let me do what I was born to do."

I watched this scene play out between Sophie and a man who was now our boss. Nothing passed between them suggested anything but friendship and guidance on his part. That made me feel better because I knew at this moment, Sophie and I would be more than that. I didn't know when or how, but my gut said more.

If my past told me anything, it was to trust my gut feelings.

Becks

"Which song do you want to start with?" I asked opening my guitar case.

"Oh, what's one you think we'll for sure be singing together?" Her face said she wanted to ask more. I couldn't understand why she was so guarded with me.

"What is it, Sophie? I know you're thinking about something."

"Well, I was lost when we rehearsed last time, and I didn't have my guitar with me. Do you think I can play my own while we go over the songs? You know, before the band gets here." Her green eyes took on a playful expression and made it impossible to say no. There was a lot more to Sophie, and she could change in an instant.

"Sure, why not? I don't know why he wanted you singing without it. Ethan knows you play."

Her eyebrows scrunched downward making a funny face. "I don't either, but I felt lost without it."

"You're used to having it between you and the crowd, too, right? Your shield?"

I watched red start up the delicious skin on her neck. I didn't mean to embarrass her. "Yeah, I'm kinda used to having it to hold on to. Did you notice me gripping the mic stand last time?"

"You mean when you white knuckled it?" I laughed hoping to end the blushing.

"Yeah, that would be the time. It makes me nervous standing there alone."

"Sophie girl, you're not alone anymore. I'll be right there beside you now. Nothing to worry about. Just you, me, and the music. Think about how stoked we'll be when we start our first song in front of a live audience."

Sophie turned and stared at me. Her green eyes now glowing with excitement. "This is really happening, Becks? I mean, we're doing this?"

"If you mean getting thousands of people pumped to hear our music, then yeah, this is really happening." Damn, I wanted to pull her in and squeeze her tight. Feeling her pressed against my body would be heaven, but now wasn't the time. Lots of rehearsal time loomed between us and that first performance. The other could wait.

"When you put it that way, I guess we do have so much to do." She adjusted the tuning on her guitar slightly. "Let's get to it."

"Right."

Glancing at the clock after what seemed minutes, I realized a couple of hours had ticked by. We managed to cover several songs until we had the sound down to precisely what I wanted. Adding the musicians to it would bump up our hard work to the next level

Becks

making it perfect for the stage. When a producer worked their magic, our EP should be epic.

"Are you happy with what we've done?" Sophie stood staring at me when I glanced back at the sound of her voice.

"Hell, yeah. They're solid now. I didn't see it before, but Ethan must have."

She sat her guitar on top of its case. "You know, it didn't make any sense to me. Your music has something so much more than mine. Your incredible vocals outshine most of the top singers today. I wondered why he wanted to add mine to yours, but now..." she took a deep breath and let it out slowly, "... I think I get it."

Sophie was right. I got it too. Our music had more unique qualities to it. Qualities that captured attention in a world saturated with great singers, great musicians. I understood Ethan now. I prayed the fans did too.

NEWS REPORT SIX

Anchor: Turning to a case we've been following now from our northeastern viewing area. Our reporter, Janna Alfred, is at the courthouse. Janna?

Reporter: I'm standing outside the county courthouse waiting to speak to the Sheriff who's been investigating a fire here in the county at the home of Judge Beckon Masters. Here he comes now. Sheriff Morgan, thank you for agreeing to speak to us today.

Sheriff: Right.

Reporter: We've been following the investigation of the fire at Beckon Masters' home. What can you tell us about the fire, Sheriff?

Sheriff: Nothing much to tell at this point. We've found some items of interest on the property, but I'm not at liberty to talk about it.

Becks

Reporter: By interesting items, are you saying there's something on the property that can help solve the mystery of the two bodies in the home?

Sheriff: No comment at this time.

Reporter: Sheriff what about the next of kin? Any luck in finding them?

Sheriff: We've not been able to locate either person. We believe they're currently on the road.

Reporter: On the road, as in running?

Sheriff: No one said running, Miss. We don't know what they're doing. I'm done here.

Reporter: Understood. Thank you, Sheriff Morgan, for the update. Back to you in the newsroom. Janna Alfred reporting from the county courthouse.

Chapter 13

SOPHIE

Laying back on my pillow, I closed my eyes. Long days and longer nights kept me exhausted. I needed a break from something. Tomorrow was my day off, but I had to spend it at the studio. We planned to practice all day since Becks had taken the time off. How many times did we do this before they deemed it perfect?

I rolled over and looked at my clock again. "No, I don't want to get up yet," I told the walls, but I knew he would bang on my door shortly since I agreed to ride in with him today. He never showed up late either—Mr. Punctuality.

Becks had a lot more going for him besides being on time. This man caused all my senses to be on high alert when I stood anywhere around him. He wore a scent that I had yet to identify—manly, woodsy, hotness all rolled into one. Identifying blindfolded would be no problem at all. Signature smells on men was a secret thing I had. Who knows, maybe my sense of smell was more alert than others.

Staring at the clock, I grimaced at the idea but got up anyway. I undressed while the water warmed, but before I stepped in the shower, a knock on my door startled me. "No way. He can't be here already. I have a good thirty minutes."

I wrapped my fluffy bright pink robe around me and started tying the belt when he started pounding on the wood frame. As cheaply as it was made, he might run his fist through it. I threw open the door to stop the banging.

"What?" That scent hit me. Well, that and clean. He must have just gotten out of the shower, splashed the goodness on himself, and drove off. Oh, God. I wanted to lick him all over he smelled so good. I stared at him as he held up a white bag.

"Donuts? They're still warm." He waved the sugary smell under my nose.

"Oh my God. Who could turn that down?" I grabbed the bag from him and turned leaving the door standing open. Getting the hint, he followed me through the den to the kitchen. I whipped around the corner in a sweet frenzy, and the knob to the cabinet door caught my robe exposing my body before I could grab it. He got a perfect body shot and typical male, he looked.

Thia Finn

"Don't look," I yelled as I pulled the soft fabric back together. The short robe barely covered my ass, and now all the goods had been on display in a hot flash of skin. I wrapped the material around me as tightly as possible and double-tied the belt this time.

"Hey, that's not fair."

I glared at him. "What's not fair? There's no free shots here, mister."

"You covered up before I got a good look, though. Teasing isn't fair."

I pushed him with my hand on his chest. "That was not a tease. That was a mistake."

"Not from where I was standing, nothing about what I saw said mistake."

I put the donuts on the counter and took the carafe to the coffee pot to fill with water. "You drink coffee, right?"

"Absolutely, but milk would be even better."

"Uh, no. Milk goes bad before I can drink it and there's nothing worse than a swallow of soured milk. Yuk."

He looked around my tiny apartment. "Were you busy when I got here or you sleep in the nude?"

"I was about to step in the shower and how I sleep is none of your business." With the button pushed to brew my favorite coffee, I turned and watched him look around. It wasn't much, but I could pay the rent without having to suffer through the whole roommate thing.

Becks

"Go ahead and shower, and I'll hang out and watch some TV that way we can go as soon as you're done."

"But the donuts." He reached in and pulled a warm, soft, glazed donut out of the bag.

"Take it with you, and you can eat the other with your coffee in the truck on the way to the studio."

"I take it you're in a hurry to get there." I took a healthy bite of the warm goodness, closed my eyes, and moaned loudly. This tasted better than anything that had passed my lips in forever. I could kiss whoever invented them.

When I opened my eyes, his were focused on my mouth. I stuck out my tongue to ring my lips and capture any of the sugar I'd left behind. Before I could, he spoke, "Here, let me." He stepped close and wrapped his palm around my jaw before he ran his thumb over my lip then put it in his mouth. The gesture was so sensual, I wanted to moan again. It couldn't have been hotter if he'd licked my lips with his own tongue. I couldn't take my eyes off his thumb as he sucked the icing off it.

"You make that look better than it tasted." His eyes dropped to my lips again. "If you take another bite, I'll remove it again."

I slowly brought the doughy confection to my lips and ran the glaze across them. This time he lowered his mouth to mine and edged his tongue over my bottom lip and then my top one, removing what I'd left on them. My breath caught in my throat at the feeling of his warm, wet tongue gliding over my lips before he pressed his lips to mine. It was soft at first, but then he moved into me, and his tongue traced the slit between my lips, seeking entrance, or sugar, I didn't care which. I opened allowing him the entrance he sought.

He leaned my head to the side to allow himself a better angle as his tongue began exploring the inside of my mouth. When we began a duel, the kiss became more crazed with teeth and tongues and lips. The taste of candied goodness heightened my need for more, and I wrapped my arms around his neck to feel his body closer to mine. His mouth pulled away from my lips, but he kissed a path down my face and jaw until he moved down my neck to the shawl collar on the robe. Damn that double knot I insisted on tying.

He dropped kisses back up the sensitive vein running up my neck to just below my ear. He nipped a bit of skin with his teeth before soothing the spot with his tongue. The bite had done its job of setting my senses on high alert, so every little hair stood down my arms and legs. I wanted to crawl up his body and wrap around him seeking pleasure that I hadn't had in forever.

Becks must have felt my senses overload because he looked back into my eyes as he rested his forehead on mine. We exchanged oxygen with our hard breathing without saying a word. I knew where I

Becks

wanted to move this, but I didn't want him to think I was desperate even if it was the truth.

Finally, I raised my head from his and without letting go of him, I eased back some. I needed to look at him. I needed to know we were on the same page. There was no reading the look he gave me, though.

Becks backed away and turned from me. "Sorry. I got carried away there."

"So did I, but it's okay."

"No, it's not okay. We're about to spend a lot of time together in each other's pockets, and I'm not sure this..." he pointed between the two of us, "... is a good idea."

"Oh." His comment surprised me. No, it shocked me. "Uh, okay. Sorry." I ran my hands up and down my arms that were crossed in front of me. "I'll just, uh... go take a quick shower. Or, uh... if you want to go ahead and go, I'll meet you there. You don't have to wait or anything."

I turned, and he caught my shoulder. "Sophie, it wasn't your fault. I didn't plan to kiss you. It just happened."

His clipped words spoke anger.

Was it directed at me?

Why would he be mad?

Did it offend him?

I nodded curtly and took off to the tiny haven. *What was I thinking allowing it to happen?* We had to work together just like he said. We needed to put this behind us and pretend it didn't happen. Was that even possible?

Chapter 14

BECKS

"What the holy fuck?" My voice echoed through the space of her kitchen. I never meant for it to go that far. She looked so damn hot standing there in the doorway in that shorter than short hot pink robe. Her toned legs smacked of perfection to be wrapped around my waist as I pounded her against the wall. It took all I had to keep my dick from going from limp to rock hard as I eyeballed her. Good thing I had the donut lifted to her face, or she might have seen the chub forming before I could get it under control.

Her robe flying open started the series of events I fought to curb. Then her moan combined with a look of ecstasy slowly extended across her face, and that ended my domination over the self-centered bastard.

He had a mind of his own and standing there watching Sophie lust over pastry ended my ability.

When the edge of her robe tickled my face, I came out of the greedy desire I harbored and landed back into reality. I wanted her badly, but I knew where this would go.

Licking her lips made me want to lick her body.

Licking her body would make me want to taste her sweetness.

Tasting her sweetness would make me want to feel her warmth strangling my dick.

It was an unlimited downward spiral into what would probably be the best sex ever, but I knew it was out of bounds for the two of us. Maybe later we could come back to this but not now. Work came first and adding sex into the music spelled disaster at this stage of the game.

I took a deep breath as I heard the shower shut off. I knew I'd hurt her by pushing her away. Better now than later, though. Women developed feelings I didn't want to deal with while we were stuck in a bus together. If one of us needed to walk away, it needed to be easy to do. Feelings enticed relationships. Steering clear of those for now made the most sense.

She stepped into the room clearly ready to leave, so I picked up her to-go coffee and the remaining confection and walked to the now open door. Sophie locked the two locks while I went ahead to the passenger door and opened it setting her remaining breakfast on the console. I moved around and got in behind the wheel and waited for her. The silence between us had to end, but I didn't want to add insult to injury, so I turned on the radio as I pulled out of the lot.

Neither of us spoke for the fifteen minutes it took to get to the building. When we walked in together, Ethan stood inside waiting for us.

"Hey, just the two I need to see." His smile said he had something good to say.

"Yeah, 'sup?"

"I've been listening to some of the music, and I think we're ready to set some tracks down. We need to put some tunes out there to see what kind of response we get." His enthusiasm caught up with me.

I turned to Sophie. "You ready for this?" My relief came when she smiled at me. I figured this girl could take a grudge to the grave, but in the studio all was forgiven, at least I hoped so.

"Sure." She directed a soft giggle at Ethan. The sweet sound made me want to hear it again, but I knew it would be pushing my luck today with how it started.

"Okay, let's do it. You two warm up and run through "Rushing to Home," and we'll get started."

I let out a whoop and passed through the doorway into the rehearsal room with her following close behind. Taking out my guitar, I fought to find the right words to say. We had to put this behind us. *Damn, why did I let it all happen today?*

"Look, Becks. About this morning. Uh... I think it's best if we forget about it and move on. You were right to stop us and about what you said. We've got a lot of time together. Handling it all in a professional manner will make our lives flow more smoothly."

"Thank God. I've been dogging myself since we got in the truck. I'm sorry. I never meant it to happen." She gave me a sad look. "I mean, not that I didn't like it because damn, woman, you're hot, but we've got a lot going on to mess it up with something like that."

"True. So, friends?" She stuck her hand out intent on shaking on it.

Shit, I hated the idea of being pushed into the friend's zone, but I could live with it, for now.

"Friends." We shook. "Okay, Sophie girl, let's do this thing."

She giggled for me this time, and all was right with my world. I prayed it was right with hers too.

For the next four grueling hours, we refined the song. Musicians showed up, and we worked with them again, then the recording process began. The excitement of hearing the raw sounds caused my adrenaline to flow. In my mind, I knew all of our practice sessions were necessary, but now tracks were being laid, and I had a whole new respect for the time Sophie, the musicians, and I spent working.

Becks

We called it quits in the late evening. Even with a lunch break, exhaustion overtook us all. I had a feeling it would be this way when we started but knowing and doing was a huge difference.

Ethan motioned to us to come in the booth he'd been in and out of all day.

"Okay. I think we've done all we can do for the day. I'm gonna say this now..." he looked over at our producer, Kevin, "... I believe we have a hit on our hands." To which Kevin smiled and nodded. "Tomorrow, I expect you both in here after work to hear the refinements."

Kevin spoke up. "Honestly, we won't be doing too many refinements because it sounded great, but there's always room for improvement in the mixing."

"True." Ethan turned back to Sophie and me. "I expect to see ya'll tomorrow with a lot to listen to."

We both nodded our heads. "We'll be here," I responded to his demand.

Walking into the studio, we loaded our gear and headed to the truck without speaking. I didn't know if she felt overwhelmed, excited, or what. I felt all of these.

As I started the truck, she finally said something. "Do you want to stop and have a beer on the way home? I know I could use one. After the day we've had, unwinding a little sounds like a good plan."

"You're right about that. I feel like I've been wound tight all day long. Let's do it."

We walked into a quiet bar the locals enjoyed hanging out in. Tourists were the last thing I wanted to spend my time with at this point. She climbed on the tall barstool and ordered a Blue Moon with orange. "I'll have the same." I'd never had one but figured it couldn't be all that bad.

"I'm exhausted, Becks." She looked through tired eyes at me.

"Yeah, me, too. I knew it would be a lot of hard work but damn, all in one day. Maybe we should have spread it out some."

"I don't think Ethan wanted to do it that way. I'm glad he tries to work around our schedules, but he'll kill me if we do this very often."

"About that. You know at some point we're going to have to give up our day jobs, right?"

"I've been saving for it. That's why I live where I do."

This came as a surprise. "Is that right?"

"Oh, you thought I enjoyed living in the worst section of town, in a run-down apartment and used public transportation for the fun of it, huh?"

"I didn't know."

"I know you didn't, and I tried hard in the beginning to keep you from finding out, but here's the truth... I wanted to do this on my own. I knew the time would come that I'd need some savings to get me through, and I figured I could suck it up and see how little I needed to live. Turns out, I don't need much."

Becks

"That's good, though, so when we start making all that money, you can enjoy living like a princess." I laughed a little.

She turned and leveled those green eyes at me. They were flecked with a brown and possibly some blue if I looked at them in the sunlight. "A princess? For real? Do I act like I need to be a princess?"

"No, but that doesn't mean when you have money you can't live like one."

"I'm not going to hold my breath on ever having enough to live that way. What about you? You want to live like a prince when you make your first million?"

"I don't know. Might be nice for a change." I swallowed down a big drink of my beer.

"Pffft. Guess we'll see."

Our conversation continued on light topics that helped us to get to know each other. We hadn't had much time alone, so I felt like this was much needed. She must have too, since she didn't suggest we leave.

The laughter between us came easily, and before we knew it, we had both drank a few too many.

"I think we did something bad." Sophie looked at her watch as she spoke.

"What's that, Sophie girl?"

"We both drank too much. How're we gonna get home?"

"Guess we'll get a ride."

"What about your truck?"

"We'll get our guitars and leave it. You ready to go?" She nodded with a funny grin on her lips. Yeah, the beer caused it.

She opened her purse and pulled out her card. "No, no. Let me buy. I got money."

Sophie cut her eyes at me. "I got money, too." Again, she giggled. "Let me buy."

"What kinda guy would I be if I did that?"

"One with money in his pocket?"

I laughed out loud. "Yep, you're right about that. I need money in my pocket. Never know when you need bail money."

"I ain't going to jail, Becks."

"Me neither, but if I did, I want bail money."

Her full laughter reached her eyes. God she was beautiful, even with beer goggles on. Wait, wasn't that what beer goggles were for? Make ugly people beautiful? I started laughing with her.

Not long after the Lyft driver pulled up to the curb and looked at the two of us. "Get out."

"Get out? Where are we?" Sophie's speech sounded jumbled to my drunk ears.

"We're where you typed in. I guess it's where you live."

Sophie looked out the window. "Oh yeah, this is me." She pulled the lever and opened the door. "Hand me my guitar, Becks."

I pushed it on the seat toward her. "There ya go, Sophie girl."

Becks

"Wait a minute," the driver called. "You gotta get out, too."

"I don't live here." I leaned back against the headrest and closed my eyes.

"Where do you live? You'll need to type it in for another ride."

"I live out this highway back there about twenty-five miles."

"Nope. I don't go out of the city. Your ride ends here, dude."

"Where am I gonna sleep?"

"Don't know. Don't care. Get out."

Sophie spoke up, "C'mon, Becks. Need to sleep."

"K." I crawled out bringing my guitar with me. "We gonna sleep together?"

"No, we're gonna sleep in the same bed."

"Oh, right. That'll work."

We both stumbled to the door.

Chapter 15

SOPHIE

Ohhh. So heavy. Something held me down, and something dug into my leg. I hadn't opened my eyes yet, but I felt the force pushing me into my mattress. The weight on my chest prevented me from taking a needed deep breath. I turned my head slightly.

Holy shit did my head hurt too.

What happened to me?

Ever so slowly, I lifted my eyelids. The act felt like an offensive chore. An arm laid across my chest, a mass of muscles hidden under dark, tanned skin.

I wiggled my hips as much as I could under the lower weight. Raising my head up, I realized a massive leg covered my thighs. I closed my eyes.

What the holy fuck did I do?

Becks

When I opened them again, I glanced to the side, and all I saw was silky dark blond hair spread everywhere. My eyes opened wider. I recognized that hair. Holy shit. Becks' mass pressed me into the mattress, his face hidden from the hair. Instantly, I knew what hurt the side of my leg. How embarrassing. Please God, let him have some clothes on. His muscled pecs were in my view, so I knew there wasn't a shirt.

I raised the covers, and thankfully, he had on some dark colored boxer briefs. *Thank you, Jesus.* At least I knew we didn't climb into bed naked, which meant we probably didn't do anything other than sleep. I wiggled my hips again and nothing down there felt sore, and since my sex life had taken a hiatus, I knew Becks and I didn't go there.

My wiggling caused him to move, but the hair continued to cover his eyes. The arm across me slid back toward him taking it's time to softly rake his palm and fingertips across my bare chest above my tank top. Good, he woke up. The large hand moved the hair from his face, and he looked at me. I wish I could hide behind some thick tresses.

Royal blue greeted me when he opened his eyes, then a brief smile which I didn't return. What the hell was he doing in my bed, and with the sun peeking through the curtains, I knew it was morning.

"Uh, Sophie?" he questioned with as much wonder as I had.

Thia Finn

"What?" I turned and stared at the ceiling. The last thing I wanted to do was look at him.

"Why am I in your bed?"

"When you remember, please tell me."

"Shit. What time is it?" He moved his heavy limbs off me and sat up but immediately laid back down holding his head. "Damn, damn, damn. What happened?"

"You sure wake up asking a lot of questions."

He reached over and looked at his phone. "Oh fuck. I'm so late for work, but damn, I don't know if I'm in any shape to go. My head is pounding."

I took this opportunity to lift the covers and see all I had on was a tank and panties. Thank God again. I needed to call in and get my evening shift covered, so I could go to the studio as Ethan asked of us but without enough clothes, I wanted to wait until he left the room.

"No need to go this late, Becks. We're supposed to be at the studio, remember?"

"Oh yeah. Dammit. I need to call Kody, like hours ago." He picked up his phone and tapped the screen. "Maybe a text would be better at this point." He typed out a brief one. "I'm sure he's figured out by now since he's finished three hours or more already."

"I have to get up," I told him as I rolled off my side and stood. Screw it. I'd slept all night this way.

"Shit." I held my head. "What did we do last night?"

"We stopped at that bar and got a ride here."

Becks

I walked into the bathroom and shut the door. I knew there was more to this story. I prayed I'd remember it the more awake I became. After going and washing my face and hands and brushing my teeth, I came back out to find Becks dressed in last night's clothes.

I grabbed my pink robe and tied it around me. This time I had other clothes so no more wardrobe malfunctions. We walked into the kitchen where two empty bottles of wine sat on the counter, along with one empty glass, one half full glass, and an empty bag of chips sitting on my small kitchen table.

"We drank two bottles of wine after all that beer? How stupid drunk were we when we got home to do something like that? We're old enough to know better."

"Yeah, my head reminds me of my age with every move. Got any ibuprofen?" He rubbed the back of his neck and up his head. His movement took the blond hair with him. *How did someone wake up looking that good?*

I pulled open a drawer and took out the bottle of generic painkillers I used, shook out two and held out my hand.

"I think I'm gonna need another."

"Three? Is that even safe?" I asked as I handed him the bottle.

"When you're head hurts like mine, more is better."

We took our meds with cold water, and I started the coffee. I needed a pot for myself. I walked to the front door and glanced out the window on the side. "Becks, where's your truck?" I turned and looked at him. I needed some answers.

"A Lyft brought us here, remember?"

"Oh yeah. He wouldn't take you home."

"Right. So we came in." He pointed to the empty bottles of wine. "What were we thinking?"

I shut my eyes. God, did it feel good. Without opening, I answered him, "We weren't. Can we go back to bed now? I need more sleep."

"Sounds good to me, but I have to get my truck."

"Whatever." I walked into the kitchen and turned off the coffee maker and went in search of my soft pillow. Before I was fully asleep, I felt the bed dip and an arm came around my middle. He spooned up against me. Right then, I couldn't have cared less, all I wanted was more sleep.

I woke with a start. Something caused it. My phone chimed. I stretched against the arm holding me.

Shit.

"Let me go."

Becks

Becks had me still pressed against him.

A text from Ethan asked what time we planned to get there today. I glanced up and saw it was already three in the afternoon. We'd slept the day away. I replied we'd both be there by four-thirty p.m. Looking over at Becks, he was on his back and shirtless again. The man needed to learn how to keep his clothes on.

No one had a right to look that good. The sheet had slipped down so his abs were now showing. Damn, I didn't think I'd ever seen someone with so well-defined muscles.

"Get up. We've gotta go."

"What?"

"It's three already. We've gotta get dressed and get your truck before we can go to the studio."

Becks sat up. "Okay. Can I shower here?"

"Sure. Lie back down, and I'll be out in a second."

"Sounds good." He was back to sleep before I shut the door. I took the fastest shower in my history, dressed, and walked out. Becks laid there looking like Adonis. Too bad I looked nothing like Aphrodite. With all that long hair and those tanned arms with muscles everywhere I looked, he could have the pick of women.

He didn't look like a bodybuilder, though. His definition showed tone but not overdone lifting like one of those guys who competed or did steroids appeared. That made me smile because being attached to some meathead on stage wasn't on my radar.

Becks must have felt my stare because his eyes opened looking straight at me. "Ogling my body, Sophie girl?" He laughed.

"How can I not. I mean, it's not every day a girl finds Mr. Muscles in her bed." I knew it insinuated what didn't happen, but flirting was okay.

He rolled on his side. "Oh really? Well, just let me know when you want to find me here again, and I'll be happy to accommodate you."

I stuck my hip out and put my hand on it. "Okay, smart-ass. Get up and shower. You'll have to put your same clothes on, though."

"I have some in my truck. I'll change when we get back to it." He stood and walked to the bathroom. "Unless you'd be willing to let me wear this fuzzy pink thing you seem to be so fond of." The robe hung on the back of the bathroom door, and he pulled the material forward for me to see against his skin.

"Uh, no. It clashes with your hair color. Now get done. We need to go."

A short time later the Uber driver dropped us at his truck in the sparsely occupied parking lot. "Guess not too many people at the bar this early."

Becks looked around as he opened his door. "Good thing since I'm about to strip." I opened the passenger door as he said it. "You're welcome to watch, though."

Becks

"Pass. You better go quickly unless you want to go to jail for indecent exposure. Cops are kinda picky here about naked men in public."

"You've seen your fair share in public?" he called as he slid his clean jeans on.

"I've seen a few down to their whitey tighties getting arrested. Something about alcohol makes your clothes fall off."

"I believe that's tequila, and it's Joe Nichols' wife, not me."

"Either way, hurry. I'd hate to have to explain you being arrested to Ethan so early in our new careers."

Becks stepped in and started the motor. "I'd hate that anytime in our long careers."

Thia Finn

NEWS REPORT SEVEN

Anchor: This just in from the field where Janna Alfred is at the Lawback County Courthouse. Janna?

Reporter: Yes, thank you, Lisa. We are here at the courthouse today to confirm that a warrant has been issued for one Becks Masters and his brother, Konan Masters.

Anchor: Do we know what the warrant is for?

Reporter: One count of arson and one of murder for each man.

Reporter: Has either been located to serve the warrant on, Sheriff?

Sheriff: Not at this time, but we expect to have them both soon.

Reporter: So the county knows where they are but hasn't been in contact with them?

Sheriff: No comment at this time. This is an ongoing investigation, Miss, and I've said all I can say.

Page | **152**

Reporter: Thank you, Sheriff. There you have it, Lisa. This is Janna Alfred reporting. Back to the studio.

Chapter 16

BECKS

"Great, you two are here. Come to my office." The three of us stepped into his domain, and he pulled a memory stick from his pocket, sat down, and popped it on his laptop. The music poured from his Audioengine speakers. I looked at Sophie. I wanted to see her initial reaction to hearing us in our first professional mode.

A slow smile crept across her lips, spread across her face, and then lit up her green opal eyes. The incredible sound flooded the office. The mix our producer worked his magic on articulated pure perfection. Sophie swayed to the sound, and the mesmerized look on her sweet face told me everything I needed to know.

Becks

As the song wound down to a stop, she leaped into my arms. "We did it, Becks. We made perfect music. I love it. I love everything about it." Her words tumbled out.

When I placed her back on the floor, we both looked at Ethan. He came around the desk and put out his hand for a congratulatory shake.

"To hell with that, man." I pulled him in for a shake and man hug before Sophie could jump up and hug him around the neck.

"Thank you. Thank you. Thank you, Ethan. You believed in us and look what we've all done. I don't know how to say the right words."

"This is only the beginning of the hard work. We're going to get you back in rehearsals to put together a full set for the clubs. We want original music, a few well-known covers, and then end with "Beyond the Words." That's step one. Next, you'll be booked into some of the local clubs and then move on from there. While this is happening, you'll be in the studio working on laying more tracks, so we can get an EP going and then a full album recorded."

"We're moving fast." Sophie's shocked face mimicked mine.

"Right. We need to strike every area. Flood the market in every aspect. We'll set up some social media accounts, Instagram, Twitter, Snapchat, and any others the PR people deem necessary to reach your demographic fan base. You'll have access to those, but

PR will want to filter your posts. We want nothing out there that is misconstrued. Also, expect to get negative feedback, too. Don't be concerned with it. So no comments."

My mind spun in circles. "Dude, that's a lot to take in at once."

"I know. I know. You worry about making great music. We'll worry about all the rest."

"What about our jobs? How will I work with all this going on?"

"Not anymore. We will advance you money."

"I won't need an advance. I've been saving every cent for when this time came," I told them both.

Sophie stuttered and blushed. "Well, I have some savings, so I'm good."

"I don't want either of you worrying about anything but doing what we ask. Like I said, you worry about making the music. We'll take care of the rest for now. Let's start by having you in the studio today to work on getting that set together. The music you've been working on all this time had a purpose."

I looked at Sophie. Her face read of doubt and surprise. "Right, let's do this, Sophie."

"Okay. I guess you're the boss, Ethan. I'm ready and thanks again." Her soft voice sounded unsure. I knew she tried to sound eager for Ethan, and maybe even for me, but we needed to show him confidence, not confusion.

Becks

I opened the door to get her out of there. "Thanks, Ethan."

"Oh, one more thing. We're sending this out to the radio stations around the country where we get guaranteed airplay. We'll have some feedback within the week. Cross your fingers."

Sophie crossed them on both hands and held them up with a smile. "Got it."

Silence filled the space between his office and the rehearsal room. Her mind probably ran a mile a minute just like mine did.

Opening the door, the musicians looked up. The drummer spoke, "About damn time." And then he smiled. They knew where we were.

They all laughed and shook hands with us. The pats on the back jumpstarted my heart and brain, making me feel better. "What do y'all think, guys? Do we have a hit on our hands?"

The bass guitar player, Jerry, spoke up looking around at the rest of the band. "Boys, do we make any fucking music here that's not platinum?" They all laughed again. I knew these guys all worked with some of the great bands that 13 Recordings produced before us.

Sophie joined them. "Now come on, Becks. They made us look good on *Beyond,*" they'll make us look good on everything. Right, guys?"

"Babe, you always look damn good. Now, we're here to make you sound the best." Jerry winked at her.

"Thanks, Jerry. Let's hope Nashville thinks the same thing."

The rest of the afternoon and into the night, we rehearsed the songs we felt would make a good set for an audience. The mix of catchy tunes and songs the fans could sing along with. We finished with four of our own to introduce to new followers hopefully. The rehearsal flew by.

Our week belonged to 13 Recordings. Everything we did had to have Ethan's and several other execs, along with the producers, approval. We decided on one of Sophie's original songs and three of mine. I had a back catalog to choose from since I wrote often. Several of them she approved of immediately. Some took a little more convincing.

Either way, we were ready to perform in the club where Ethan booked us. He wanted our first night to be small, so we could fine tune for the next location, which held three times the people. On Saturday, Ethan scheduled us to open for another band from the label. I felt lucky they happened to be in town because their huge following in Nashville meant we'd be getting quality exposure.

Becks

The closer the day of the show came, the more nervous Sophie seemed. After witnessing her little meltdown at the open-mic night, I watched her closely to see if we might be dealing with it again.

"Sophie?" I called when we headed out for the day after our last real rehearsal before the show.

"Yeah?" She stopped and turned to me. Her pale face worried me.

"You okay?" I touched her arm. After that kiss we'd shared, I swore I wouldn't go there again but touching her delicate skin caused the memory of it to resurface like a wrecking ball sledged through a solid brick wall.

She turned her green eyes up to me. "Sure. I'm great. How could I be otherwise?" Her voice had a soft feel to it, not the conviction it usually had.

I leaned against the hallway wall turning her to face me. "Let's see. We're about to start our career for real. We've practiced night and day for what seems like months now. Our sleeping and eating habits are shit. Yeah, how the hell could we be anything but great?"

"When you put it like that, Becks, maybe I need to rethink what I said." She wrapped her arms around herself. The defensive move told me she tried to keep it all in. I wanted to gather her in my arms and reassure her the show's success was a non-issue but knew it might be the wrong thing to do.

"Sophie, it's going to be the best damn show of our lives. I can feel it."

She stared up at me. "You can't know that, Becks."

"Yeah, I do. I trust my instinct on this stuff." She gave me a look that told me she didn't believe a word I said.

"That's good from your side, but that doesn't mean it'll be that way for me, too." This girl exuded confidence when it came to everything else. *Why did she shy away now?*

"It does, Sophie girl. We got this. Take my word for it." Still disbelief. Fuck it. I pulled her to me in a tight hug. We both needed it. "We can do this. I know we can. You need to start telling yourself this, right now. Say the words. We've got this."

Nothing.

"We've got this. We've got this. Say it, Sophie. We've got this," I kept repeating it.

Finally, she said it with me. "We've got this."

"Again."

"We've got this."

"Again."

She repeated the phrase several more times.

"Well?" I questioned.

"Well, what?" She scrunched her eyebrows up the way she did.

"Do you believe it, yet?"

Her shoulder lifted. "I guess. It's just scary thinking we'll be singing in front of a full room."

Becks

"But you've done this before, Sophie. What's different? We've even sung a little together, remember?"

"Yes, I know, but before I sang other people's music. I imitated what great singers did. Now you're asking me to sing our music."

"We'll be singing a lot of different music. Others' hits. My songs. Your songs. They'll all be the same."

"No, Becks they won't be the same. What if our songs don't work?"

"They will, Sophie girl. They will. Do you think the label would promote us if they thought we couldn't positively represent them? Their rep says everything. If we fuck up, they look like shit, too. They're not going to let us. Did you even consider that?"

She looked down at her feet and shook her head. "No, I didn't think about it that way." I raised her head to look at me again. "I guess they think we have some talent."

"Some talent? Sophie, together we have so much talent to shine with, the crowd's ideas of greatness will shoot into tomorrow." My enthusiasm climbed with each word. "We're going to be the next best thing on the music scene. You just wait, Sophie girl."

We walked side by side to the parking lot. "Hop in. I'll take you home after we grab some supper."

"I don't think I can eat, Becks. My stomach's too nervous."

"All the more reason we should do it then. Maybe you'll forget about everything for a while. Let's talk about everything but music." We stopped at my truck, and I opened the passenger door for her.

She stared at me for a full minute, then climbed in.

I leaned toward her. "Good thing you made the right choice. I'd have hated having to physically put you in here. We'd start all kinds of rumors for the paparazzi." I made a point of looking up. "Look, there they are now." I ducked my head behind the door pretending to hide. "Oh no, there's another in the bushes. Hide girl." I squatted down beside her seat and pulled the door to me. "Damn, guys," I yelled. "Get a real job." By the time I finished pretending to dodge the hated photographers, Sophie's laughter could be heard to the building.

"You're crazy. Did you know that?"

I stepped in the driver's seat and started the motor. "No, but don't say it loud. Those guys will print anything." I loved hearing her laugh. The sweet tinkling sound made my heart skip a beat because it didn't happen very often.

Something, or someone, needed to change that. I vowed to make it happen as much as possible when we went on tour.

Chapter 17

SOPHIE

As I read the online reviews of our first night on stage, I thought about all the fun we had. The show turned out just as Becks had promised. Perfect.

Before we went on, Becks made me repeat his mantra over and over again. I said it to myself when we stood behind the mics. I guess it did the trick to get me in the right head space because we started the first song, and I didn't miss a beat.

The audience's cheers and hurrahs kept my nerves at bay and more, it gave me the courage to let go and be a performer in every sense of the word. I rocked to the music while we sang. After the first song, I handed off my guitar to the stagehand, so I could have more freedom to move to the music.

Thia Finn

Turns out, I really liked dancing around while I sang our alt-rock music. I got into it, and before I knew what was happening, our last song, "Beyond the Words," was up. Becks introduced it, and when he said the name, the audience went a little crazy.

Ethan landed the song a lot of airtime on all the local rock stations that week, so when we broke out into the chorus, the audience knew the words. I looked at Becks with my eyebrows touching my hairline in surprise. That was a first. My excitement level escalated through the roof. I had to calm down—but in a good way—to sing the song. My stage fright was a thing of the past, and I prayed it would stay there.

As the song came to an end, the people went wild with shouts and praises for our music. We waved and yelled to them before finally leaving the stage. Becks took off his guitar backstage and picked me up instead, twirling me around like I weighed nothing. In our adrenaline-filled excitement, I don't think I did. Instead, I floated above the floor.

Ethan and our producer stood backstage watching us and shouting praises of their own. I hugged them, too. Hell, I hugged everyone in the band, the guys backstage, whoever stood around got a hug or a hand slap.

The entire group migrated to the bar to have drinks. A few people came over for pictures and autographs, which we gladly gave them.

Becks

My autograph.

Who would have ever thought someone would feel I was important enough for giving an autograph?

I bounced around in my seat of Becks' truck on the way home. I couldn't seem to calm down even after two drinks. After the last beer slash wine fiasco, we both declined a third one.

"I just don't think I'll be able to sleep tonight. Maybe I should've had that third drink."

Becks laughed at me. "You'll crash pretty soon. When the adrenaline drains, you'll bottom out with exhaustion."

"Pooh, you make it sound like a bad thing."

"Pooh? Really?" He laughed again. "I love it when you finally let go and be yourself instead of uptight and guarded all the time."

I looked at him hard in the darkness of the truck. "I'm not guarded, I'm careful."

"Call it what you want. After seeing you tonight on stage, I know a whole new you."

"Yeah, I was having an awesome time."

"It showed, all the dancing around and playing with the audience you did. You made it look like you've done this all of your life."

"I guess it was easy to do knowing you were there with me."

"Oh, so you're saying that I calm you so you can be the real you?"

"Your mantra, I repeated it over and over. I kept saying it, you know, once we were behind our mics, too."

"Good. I'm glad it helped because that's the you I want to see all the time, especially on stage."

If I didn't know better, I would think he wanted to see me that way in bed too. The way he looked at me when he said it. The way his eyes had bedroom written all over them. The look on his lips said kiss me. Right at that moment, I wanted to do more than kiss him.

Whew, this adrenaline thing might prove dangerous on a tour bus. I needed to be careful. He'd already said the way he felt about anything happening between us, so I knew nothing was going to come of my needs with him. Guess I'd be taking care of myself again tonight. Thank goodness for new batteries.

Something was just wrong about having sex-toy sex when I'd been with a hot guy half the night. What a confidence killer.

Becks turned in the space in front of my apartment, and I gathered my things. He came around and opened my door, holding my guitar case. "Come on. I'll help you get it all inside."

I nodded and stepped out. He stood close enough behind me as I unlocked the lock that I could feel his breath where I'd wound my hair up from my neck after our set. The warmth sent electricity down me.

Becks

Not fair, Becks. My motor's revved up enough already, I didn't need hot, sweet breath brushing over my skin.

He didn't back up as I turned around to get my things, so we were toe to toe. "Uh, I guess I'll see you tomorrow unless you want to come in."

"Depends."

I cocked my head a little, "Depends?"

"Yeah, do you want me to stay the night or go because I know if I get inside, this is going to head into new territory. If you don't want that, then I need to say goodnight right here on your doorstep and go."

I dropped my bags, fisted his shirt front to pull him to me, rose up on my toes, and kissed him. I heard my guitar case hit the ground, but I didn't care because his arms wrapped around me with his big hands splayed across my back. They pulled me tightly against him. God, it felt good to touch his taut body that way.

I might have started the kiss, but when he took over, he finished it, but not before he thoroughly owned my lips, teeth, cheeks, and tongue. His tongue licked and lavished every possible inch of my mouth. When my tongue slipped passed his, and into his mouth, he sucked it in and played with it in the most delicious way I'd ever experienced. By the time he broke the kiss, I gasped for air. God, this man could kiss, and I knew I hadn't had nearly enough to satisfy me, so I pulled him forward as I walked backward. He slammed my door shut with his foot and one hand left me long enough to throw the deadbolt.

He spun us around and backed me into the door where he took my lips again ravaging every sense I had, then started across my cheek and down under my ear. He bit and nipped his way to the curve of my neck, and I groaned a soft sound when he bit at my collarbone. My hands found the soft strands of hair that had slipped from his ponytail. I pulled it all from the leather tie. I wanted to run my fingers through every inch of the softness. When he nipped at my skin, I wrapped it around my fingers and pulled, creating brief moments of pain just like he'd left on my neck. Exchanging the quick stings sharpened the need between my legs.

As he started back up to my ear, he spoke softly between bites. "I wanted to wait until we were on the bus before anything happened between us."

"How did you know it was going to happen?" I managed to get out as I felt myself begin to completely melt under his lips.

"I've told you before, I know these things. I can just feel them." His warm breath and tongue heated my insides as he sucked my earlobe into his mouth and bit it softly, pulling it between his teeth as he slid off the edge. His tongue continued up the outer edge of my ear, skipping over the several piercings in it.

Becks

"Is that right? Kinda like I'm feeling things now?" I ground my hips into the raging hard-on he worked against me.

When he pushed me harder with his body against the door and ran his thickness against my cleft, I was ready to detonate. It had been a long time since a man had given me an orgasm, and my body ached for the release. For the connection it brought. For the feeling of warmth it created. Right now, I wanted this man to make it happen.

He slid his hands to my ass and lifted me, wrapping my legs around him, kissing me all the way to my bed. He fell forward trapping me under him. God, it felt... felt... my brain couldn't describe it. The heat, the friction he created. My first real orgasm grew, and he hadn't even gotten my clothes off.

With a short skirt on, lifting me brought it up around my waist, so his jeans and my red panties were all that kept us from being skin to skin. I wanted skin. I dreamed of skin. His skin, touching mine.

"Can we lose the panties?" His request answered my prayers.

"Yeah, if we can lose the jeans." He stood and wrapped a finger under each side of my underwear, sliding it down my body. When he got to the red heels I wore, he slipped them over the shoes. "I think we'll keep these, though. Damn, they've been driving me crazy all night watching you dance around in them. All I could think about was them sliding up and down my thighs and across my back when you wrapped me in these silky legs."

I rose up and pulled my shirt over my head tossing it across the room where he'd thrown my panties.

"Mmm... red on your pale skin looks good enough to eat." He leaned down pushing me back to the bed. "I think I will." He ran his tongue across the tops of my breasts that begged to be released. As he started back across, his tongue dipped in far enough to tease my taut nipple.

"Ohhh. Yes, please." That's all it took for him to reach up and pull the red lace down enough to free the aching flesh. He ran his tongue around the tight skin before his teeth scraped from base to point.

Writhing below him, I needed more so I reached to his jeans he'd managed to keep on. I popped the button open and slipped my hand inside to find the warmth I sought. The head on his swollen cock had a bead of pre-cum waiting. I slid my index finger through the drop, smearing it around the tight skin.

"Sophie girl. Let's take them off. Now." His words exposed the desperation in his voice. I pulled the zipper down ready to help, but he stood, pushed them off, stepping out of his boxers and jeans together. Leaning over, he pulled my skirt off and popped the hook between my breasts taking the time to slide it down my arms and tossing it over his head.

"Condom in the nightstand drawer."

Becks

He pulled one out throwing it beside me. "You're so perfect, Sophie." He kissed up my stomach. "I can't wait any longer to be inside you." He stopped and bit and kissed around my nipples again causing me to wrap my legs around him digging the heels into his ass to get him where I wanted him to be.

He pulled back and ripped open the condom, wrapping the hard length I hadn't had time to explore yet. His eyes on mine. I watched his actions. "Later." Reaching down between my legs, he lightly ran his finger up my entire length but didn't breach the crevice. "This looks like heaven."

"But you're putting me through hell."

Becks smiled up at me. "Not for long." His finger slipped past the seam, and he it slid inside me dragging the waiting rush of liquid up to my clit where he circled it over and over without actually touching it.

I cried out when I couldn't take the torture any longer. "Do something. I'm dying."

He ran his swollen cock in the same path his finger had taken before popping my clit with it. I froze up. My toes curled under, my legs went rigid, and I came, hard. Never before had I orgasmed from light taps.

"Becks," I moaned as he pushed inside me. Not hard the first time, but since I hadn't come down from the climax yet, my sensitivity was on high alert. He pulled back out and then took me hard, bottoming out, with his pubic bone hitting my clit. I came again.

"Oh God. Becks, Becks, Becks," I screamed out in pleasure. I'd never had sex feel like this before. He knew exactly where to rub, where to hit, where to touch. He did it over and over until he sat back on his calves, still inside me.

"Come for me again, Soph. Once more. Squeeze my dick tight. Let me feel you come all over it." He did the thing again popping my clit, this time with his finger as I was spread wide open for him. I started coming, and he took my hips in his hands and pulled me down his dick over and over. From this angle, his swollen cock rubbed the rough patch that set me off into another mind-bending orgasm. This time, though, he came too, yelling unintelligible sounds as he drove into me. I felt the warmth inside me as he filled the barrier between us.

Becks leaned over kissing each of my breasts softly before taking my mouth in a kiss that would have left me needy if he wasn't still buried inside me. When he sat up, he pulled out and stood to remove the condom that he disposed of in the bathroom.

He returned to find me stuck in the same position. My body refused to move, or maybe my rendered, thoughtless mind refused to send the signal.

He crawled up beside me. "You okay, Sophie girl?"

My eyes changed positions looking at this beautiful, naked man and an easy smile spread across my lips. No words exchanged between us, though. He rolled me on my side and moved in behind me, leaving no space between our spent bodies. After pulling the covers around us from the side of the bed, he wrapped his arm around my middle with his fingers spread across my stomach. His little finger rested just above my well-used pussy as though he kept it safe.

Sleep won over consciousness and blissfully took me under thinking I was safe.

Chapter 18

BECKS

"Goodnight, Nashville." Each show ended on a high heightened by the screams and shrieks from our audiences wishing us night after night of good fortune. Most nights my own mind couldn't wrap around what our lives became in such a short time.

Just as Ethan promised, the label's PR people promoted our every move for the next month. In and around the Nashville area, venues now sought us for their stages. Word spread of our talent and music with wildfire speed.

Sophie peeked out from the stage wing at our show the next night while the roadies changed the first band's equipment. "This is really happening, isn't it?"

I stepped in behind her peering over her head to watch the chaos in the pit section of the indoor slash outdoor club. With VIP off to the side, people stood directly in front of the stage. I loved this. Having them so close, we felt their energy and fed off it. The more they gave us, the harder we worked to match it.

"Yeah, it's happening all right. But damn, I had no idea our success would be this fast."

"Me either." She glanced over her shoulder and formed a slight smile. "I suppose after playing for such a long time in dive bars to barely interested customers, I assumed our shows would be the same."

"We have to give Ethen and his crew credit for this. He told us to be ready for it. Guess he knew what he was talking about."

"They do deserve it, but then, it's his job to know. Thank God he's good at his job." We both laughed before moving to our marks on stage to perform another set to an enthusiastic audience.

The night we spent together met all of my expectations too, but we hadn't had a repeat performance of it. I knew our time together was about to be twenty-four seven, so I backed off and didn't push for any kind of closeness with Sophie. Sending mixed signals wasn't really my style, but too much too soon might cause problems later on down the road.

We finished laying the tracks for the EP Ethan wanted, and everyone praised the finished product. Once again, the label pushed it toward all the right people, and we started receiving the kinds of reviews that made bands known.

The reviews read like a dream. Only one female reviewer spent her time talking about the band behind us more than the songs and lyrics, which was okay. They needed love too. Their musical abilities made us look even better than we were, in my opinion, so I gladly shared the spotlight with them on her blog.

Radio interviews began too. They asked planned questions. PR still wanted to control the responses, but occasionally, the listeners called in with them. Spontaneous answers scared the shit out of us both with all the warnings we were given.

DJ (Cade): Thanks for getting up at the ass crack of dawn to be here, SoBeck.

Becks: Oh no, we're happy to be here. Especially Sophie. She's always wide awake early." *Becks and DJ laugh.*

Sophie: *Sleepy voice.* Yeah, I'm such a morning person. *More laughter in the studio.*

DJ: So you guys exploded on the Nashville rock scene. How does it feel to know your first single reached the top ten?

Becks: You know, Cade, we're both excited to see it all happening quickly. "Beyond the Words" reaching top ten is unrealistic still. We only dreamed about something so mind-blowing could happen to us.

Becks

Sophie: We still can't get a wrap on it. I mean, how did that happen?

DJ: I see lots of callers have questions. Would you like to take some?

Becks: Sure, why not?

Line One: So, I was at your show last night. Becks, you're so hot. Are you and Sophie, like you know, doing the nasty or is it just a basic? *Sophie turned to me with a WTF face.*

Becks: Well, we are definitely friends if that's what you want to know. We, uh... well, we don't really see each other outside the studio and while we're working.

Sophie: Right. We don't do any kind of bumping, so I guess you would say we're keeping it basic.

DJ: Caller two, you're up.

Line Two: Hey, just wanted to say how glad I am to get to see you when you're building your crowd. I'm always willing to support new bands, and you two have a great sound.

Sophie: Thank you so much. We're are excited to have people who are willing to support us right now. Being new is kinda hard, but we look forward to meeting some of you soon at a concert.

Line Three: So, Becks, the way you swing that long hair around on stage drives me and my friends craaazzzyyy. Please don't ever cut it.

Becks: Not a problem. I mean, I get a trim once in a while, but my long hair is a part of me that I'm not going anywhere without. Besides what would Sophie pull on when she's mad and wants to hurt me?

Line Three: Oh no she doesn't. I'll cut a bitch for that. *Disconnect.*

DJ: Right, well, I think we need to let these two get out of our studio. Thank you both for crawling out so early. I know the listeners are happy to know you're doing a few more shows here in Nashville before heading out.

Becks and Sophie: Yeah, thanks for having us. We appreciate the station for playing our music and coming to the shows.

DJ: Okay, listeners, that's SoBeck. Check their website for their last show before they head out on their first tour.

The DJ started a tune and stood. "Really appreciate you both being here. I know these fucking early morning hours are lame."

I shook his hand. "Yeah, it's early for us, but Sophie girl and I are always glad to be here. You know, the more exposure at this point, the better."

"Right. We're happy to make appearances." Sophie caught herself from yawning in his face.

The DJ laughed. "Think you better take her back to bed, dude." We both looked at him. "I mean, you know,

Becks

like wherever y'all sleep." His innocuous comment caused a little embarrassment. Sophie's face turned a bright shade of blushing red.

"It's all good." I waved at him and moved toward the doorway. "We're going to probably hear that kind of comment a lot."

As the elevator doors closed, Sophie turned on me. "What the fuck, Becks? You can't go around telling people like him those kinds of things."

"What was I supposed to say, Soph? He knew he messed up as soon as he said it. Did you see his face?"

"No, I was too busy hiding behind my mortification. You know what the PR people would say if they found out."

"I don't give a shit what they find out. We're grown-ass adults, Sophie. If we want to sleep together or with a hundred fans, it's none of their damn business." The door opened, and our conversation screeched to a halt.

After walking out the double glass doors, she picked it up again. "I just hope Ethan doesn't hear about it."

"So what if he does, Sophie? I'm not ashamed of having a relationship with you. I mean, we don't really have a relationship like that, but we could, and I don't give a single fuck who knows about it." I opened her door. "Wait a minute... are you saying you are embarrassed?"

She stared at me without answering.

My door slammed harder than I wanted. Being mad about this wasn't the way to start. I put the key in the ignition but didn't start the motor. "Well?"

"Well, I don't know what to say. I mean, we kissed and then you tell me no we can't do this. We fuck and nothing's even different between us. Are we gonna be like fuck buddies or something while we're on tour?"

I didn't have a comeback to her words. The deadpan look I gave her must have said it all.

"So that's what you want? I'm not sure I'm down with that, Becks. I'm not really cut out for meaningless sex."

"There was nothing meaningless about what we did. It was mind-blowing sex, Sophie."

She gazed straight ahead, and then her lips turned into a grin. "Yeah, it was pretty hot, but still, I thought we started something. Then you move on like everything's the same, Becks."

The motor roared to life when I turned the key. "We need to think about this, Sophie girl. Is it really what we want?"

She looked at me and then turned her head to stare out the window all the way to her place. When I stopped in front of the apartment, she bailed out and slammed the door before running inside.

I watched to see if she might come back, but after a few minutes, I backed out and went to the other side of Nashville. A new place to live happened faster than expected. I wanted to wait until we came back from

Becks

the short tour but driving back and forth thirty miles got old.

I picked up my phone and dialed. Kody's phone only rang once when he answered. "Hey, Becks. What's up?"

"You got plans?"

"Nope. Nothing going on here," he said opening a beer can. The pop and fizz sound came through the phone.

"I'm coming to get my stuff to move to my new place. Thought you might want to come hang."

"Dude, you don't have anything but clothes and all that shit in the bathroom you put in your hair. I'll gather it up and bring it, so you don't have to make the trip out here."

"That'd be great, but I wanted to talk to your mom and dad. I owe them both a lot for letting me stay and the job and all."

"Send them a signed album or something. It'll thrill them to see your name on it."

"Yeah, I'll do that, too, but it's not the same as telling them in person. Be there in thirty. You can follow me back."

"No show tonight?"

"No, got a night to regroup."

"We gonna see Sophie?"

"Probably not. She's on the other side of town now."

Page | **181**

"What'd you do, Becks? Your voice says something's shaky in paradise."

"We're fine. She's just tired and trying to wrap her head around all this shit we're doing."

"Understandable."

"See you in a few."

The ride to Kody's house left me too much thinking time. My past sneaking up and biting me in the ass could happen at any moment, especially if I stuck around in one place. The tour needed to start, yesterday.

The situation wasn't on me, but I knew more than I needed to know. Putting it all off as long as possible suited me just fine.

"You don't be a stranger now, Becks. We'd love to see you from time to time," Kody's mom patted me on the shoulder, and I leaned in and kissed her cheek before leaving. This lady had as much in common with my own mom as a gun and a knife. They were both women, and that's where it ended.

"I appreciate all you and Randy did for me while I was here. If it weren't for your family, I'd probably be living under a bridge down by the river."

Becks

"Oh, son, we'd have never allowed that." Her eyes twinkled with the truthful knowledge.

I shook Randy's hand. "Thanks again, sir. For everything."

Randy looked hard into my face as if he wanted to say something and then stopped. "You take care. Don't be a stranger. Makes Annette feel left out." He turned and walked away.

His words weren't lost on me. This big man had a soft heart even if he rarely showed it. "I'll do that, sir. No way I want Mrs. Richards mad at me," I called after him. He raised his hand in the air in way of waving and walked into the house.

"Well, you get on into Nashville before it gets too late. Don't want to worry about y'all on the road after dark."

I smiled. Only a parent would think of something like that. Looking at Kody. "You ready?"

"Yeah, let's yeyo."

"What?"

"You know... go, leave."

"Someone's been spending too much time on Urban Dictionary again." I laughed stepping into my truck. "I gotta errand I have to do before I can go home," I yelled to where he sat in his own vehicle.

"What's that?"

"I gotta go get my driver's license changed."

"Today?"

"Yes, today. The label people want this done asap so we can sign shit. I'll give you the key to my place, and you can wait there. Oh, and stop and get some beer, too. Nothing in my fridge yet."

"I knew this trip would cost me."

"Call it a housewarming gift for my first place." My snorting laughter earned a funny look.

A short drive later, I arrived at the DMV where they picked my birth certificate apart. Since I didn't have my old license and conveniently couldn't remember the number, they needed another form of ID. It read Becks O'Donnell as it did when my mother bought the copies.

Finally deciding it was legit, they issued one to my new address, and I took off before they asked any more questions. I'd have the plastic one in seven days, but the paper one would work for 13 Recordings. Sophie took care of this the first day, but I wanted to get this information all straight before I signed anything important.

Chapter 19

SOPHIE

"No, Mom. Everything's going great." The label will advance me money when I run out if we haven't started bringing in royalties. Talking to my mom about money gave me a migraine. She never cared before, so why did she bother to ask now? Always the same thing. Money. Maybe she needed more and counted on me making it big to share mine with her. Never going to happen. Not in this lifetime.

"You know your dad and I will send you money, Sophie. You don't have to do this alone."

"Yes, I do. I need to prove I can. Besides, Becks and I are going to write some music together, and then I'll make even more from the royalties because I'll be the singer-songwriter."

"I thought you said you'd already written songs."

"I have, Mother, but we're only using one of them. The rest are Becks'. At least, so far."

"You plan to have more for us to hear?"

"Yes, Mother. When the LP comes out, it'll have several of my songs on it." At least I hoped it did.

"Okay, if you're sure, honey. We don't want to see you get taken by those men running the show."

"It's not all men. There are women in this company, too." At least I thought there were. I hadn't actually thought about it.

"I gotta run. Our manager wants me to shop for clothes better suited to our image."

"Oh, so you have an image now." The lightness in her voice said she joked, but the truth was the execs wanted me to change for appearances. I like comfortable. They liked edgy.

"I have to look the part, Mom."

"Call when you can, honey."

"Yes, Mom. Love you."

"Love you, too."

I missed my parents, but proving I had what it took was personal. I opened my laptop and pulled up some of the sites the label wanted me to shop from.

"Yeah, uh, no. I'm not wearing these things."

My doorbell rang, and I peeked out seeing a woman standing there. I expected someone, but this wasn't it. Opening it, I stuck my head out. "May I help you?"

"Are you Sophie Turner?"

"Yes."

Becks

"Well, chica... I'm here to help you."

"Help me what?"

"Buy new clothes, bitch." I backed away and opened the door wider.

"Okay." Who was she to call me a bitch?

"Oh no. You're looking at the pathetic sites they told you about." She picked up my laptop and closed it. "Forget those places. We're going shopping."

"Where?" I stared at her dress. She wore a blue floral print maxi dress that was backless and tied at the neck to keep the ruffled cap sleeves from sliding over smooth shoulders. Her long blonde hair waved perfectly down her tanned back. She looked Cali ready. I looked couch ready, yoga pants and Nirvana t-shirt.

"Everywhere. You need clothes for the stage, for meet and greets, for interviews."

"I have clothes for some of that already."

"Not according to the power boys."

"The power boys?"

"You know, the ones who think they make all the decisions. When in reality, we make all the decisions about how to dress, perform, live. You know. Now, come on. Get dressed and let's go."

I looked down at myself. "I thought I was dressed."

"For sitting around the house, bitch, but not for shopping. Put on something fun and let's boogie."

Boogie? Who said that? Apparently, wait. I didn't even know her name. "Uh, you never told me your name."

She stuck her hand out. "Oh sorry. I'm so stoked to redo your image, I forgot. I'm Monet Fields. You know, like the painter?"

Okay. "Nice to meet you, Monet."

"Yeah, my parents spent a lot of time at the Met when they were pregnant with me. Apparently, cheap and air-conditioned fit the bill." She plopped down on my couch. "Now get ready. Time's a wasting."

After quickly getting dressed, we headed to the car. She drove to shops I didn't even know existed in Nashville. They sold bohemian clothes, and for me a true love was born. Other shops selling interesting styles for the stage stood side-by-side with the new boho styles I wanted. Monet found a skin-tight leather skirt and a flowy dress that was so short, the color of my panties would never be a mystery in either. The dress would be off limits on stage.

Boots that laced and sky-high heels added to the bill. My favorite outfit looked like a sexy sports bra with a thigh-length, laser-cut black tank over some skinny black jeans. Against my lily-white skin, I fell in love. Stiletto heels perfectly finished the look. Prayers would be said before walking on stage in these babies.

I felt like Cinderella got to shop in her rocker stepsisters' closets. I'd never had so much fun. Monet laughed at me several times, but we bought so many

Becks

different looks, so I could change it up daily. With our last show in Nashville coming up and heading out on the road, I'd look and feel the part.

"I wonder what Becks will think about all this." I held out my arms covered in shopping bags for Monet.

"He'll be like, 'damn girl, who are you?'" Her laughter felt contagious when I joined her. "Besides, do you care what he thinks?"

"Yeah. I want him happy on stage."

"If this clothing recon doesn't catch some positive attention, the boy is stooopid." The comment doubled me over laughing. "I'm so right, right?" I nodded since I couldn't speak. "When am I going to meet the fabulous new star, Becks?"

"Fabulous, huh? I don't know about all that."

"Chick, if I could meet him long enough to run my fingers through his hair, I'd die one happy bitch."

"Haha. That's real funny." How did Becks' hair always become a topic of conversation? When we talked to fans after the shows, it was a guarantee his hair would become part of the conversation.

She ran her fingers through her own hair. "It looks soft and thick and..."

"Perfect for touching?" I added.

"Yes, that, too. What I'd like to do is wrap it around my hand and pull him in for a big ol' juicy kiss with it."

"Eww. That sounds like dominatrix talk." I smiled as I said it, but honestly, the idea of her kissing Becks caused me to feel a little jealous. I didn't do jealous.

Thia Finn

Ever. Either he was mine one hundred percent, or he wasn't. Trust shouldn't be an issue. As far as I was concerned, trust and jealousy were connected. If I was jealous, then I didn't trust him.

"Hell yeah, it is. I'd like to find myself a bad boy who likes to be dominated."

I couldn't help myself, I had to give her a hard look as we put my bags in her trunk. "Really? You want a guy you always have the upper hand with?"

"Maybe not always, but sometimes I'd like to be the boss. You know, take charge in the bedroom. Have them do as I say. That would be one badass night."

"Since you're still dreaming, I'm assuming you haven't found one yet."

She turned in the parking space at my place. "No, not yet but that doesn't mean I'm not always looking."

"Wine?"

"Always." She laughed.

My phone rang before I could get out. "Speaking of long, blond, non-dominate males... hey, Becks."

"Hi." After our conversation last night, I didn't exactly know what I wanted to say to him. What I didn't want to do was allude to last night's argument in front of Monet.

"I wanted to talk, but I'm headed to my new place, and Kody's going to be there. You should come over. I'm still out, so I can swing by and get you."

I looked at Monet. Our time shopping had been fun, and I wasn't ready for it to end. "You want to head

Becks

over and see Becks' new place? We can take the wine with us." She replied with an 'are you even asking' look.

"Okay if I bring a friend with me? We'll bring our own wine."

"Sure. Sounds great. Is he a neighbor or something?" Good, serves him right to wonder about me.

"Uh, not exactly." Let him keep wondering. "Text me the address."

"Oh my God. This is too funny. I won't be able to look at him without thinking about his hair now."

"Forget it. He's definitely not interested in being dominated."

"And you'd know this how? Bitch, are you telling me you've already tried it?"

"No, I've not tried wrapping his hair around my fist."

She grabbed my arm. "But your hair's been around his fist? Please tell me it has." She didn't seem bothered by the idea that we'd hooked up already, but then she had no way of knowing our backgrounds.

"His hands might have been in my hair a time or two." I felt the need to keep some of it still a mystery. I'd chided him for speaking of it already, and here I was spilling my guts to a new person who worked for the label, no less. Damn, I'm such a hypocrite. I didn't have many friends here in Nashville, and since I'd quit, I never got to see Andi anymore.

Page | 191

"No fucking way," she shouted in the confines of her car. I didn't answer with anything but a smile while still facing straight ahead. She slapped my arm this time. "Damn, bitch. Why didn't you tell me this to begin with? We'd have bought some super sexy lingerie to go under all these things."

"I don't need to wear sexy lingerie on stage."

"Chica, I didn't say a damn thing about while you were on stage. I'm talking about when he peels these clothes off your sweaty body in a janitor's closet after you come off stage. I've seen the shape those guys are in when they come off stage high from the crowd's excitement and band-craze."

"Band-craze? Where do you get these words?"

"You know what I'm talking about. Fans going all wild for the band and are ready to do obscene things to those hot, sweaty guys. Don't you feel the same way when you and Becks see each other coming off stage?"

"Maybe." I had but didn't want to say it out loud because then I'd have to admit it to myself.

BECKS

Two smoking hot females stood outside my door, each with a bottle of wine. What more could a guy ask for? Must be my lucky day.

"Well, hello ladies." I used my best sleazy voice. They both laughed, exactly what I was going for. This night would be a lot more fun keeping things light. Having a friend with her, Sophie's topics of conversation wouldn't include last night's fiasco. That conversation needed to happen another time.

"We brought refreshments." They both held up their bottles.

"Always the best kind of guests." I put my hand out for them to come in.

"We'd call it a housewarming gift, but since we plan to drink it ourselves, it's more of a gift to us." They both laughed. Had they started on it before coming here? I rarely saw this easy side of my partner.

"No problem." I held my beer up. "I'll stick to this. The last time we mixed the two didn't turn out so well."

Sophie stared into my eyes. With this, 'don't go there' stare or 'it's funny, do share' stare? "You going to introduce me to your friend, Sophie girl?"

"This is Monet Fields." Sophie pointed between Kody and me. "Monet, this is Becks O'Donnell and Kody Richards. Monet works for 13 Recordings. Kody and Becks used to work together. Okay, now we all know each other."

Kody spoke up. "You make us seem so unimportant, Sophie." He stood and pulled her in for a side hug. "Now you know Becks and I are actually your part-time bodyguards." He leaned toward Monet. "We bring the muscle when she's in distress."

"More like hide in the truck causing me a panic attack," Sophie added.

"Now come on, Sophie. We weren't hiding that night in the bar when that big bastard couldn't keep his hands off you."

"True." She turned to Monet. "They can be useful in certain situations."

Kody couldn't resist. "I can be more than 'useful' in certain situations." He air-quoted the word.

Monet broke into laughter. "I bet you can. Are you in the music business, too?"

Becks

Now it was my turn to laugh. "Uh, that would be a big *no*. The guy can do anything with a saw and a hammer but can't sing worth shit."

"That's not fair, you've never heard me with a microphone."

"Dude, a microphone, a full orchestra, and the best damn backup singers in the world couldn't change your ability to sing."

By the time the evening ended with the light banter and relaxed laughter and maybe slight intoxication, we'd created a new group of friends. Sophie and I hadn't had the opportunity before this to simply hang out and get to know each other this way. Our time had always been taken up with work, coming and going to work, or intimately.

Watching her with others, laughing, telling stories, and effortlessly having fun gave me a chance to see a side of her I loved. No stress existed in the room, and her relaxed nature made my feelings for her something I wanted more of. We skipped this important step along the way. Friendship, with someone I was about to spend a lot of up-close-and-personal time, seemed a requirement if we were going to create a lasting bond.

If our relationship continued in bed, then getting to know each other as friends was even more important to me. A connection had to more than about fucking. A link like that would never last, and since we were entering a partnership, more nights like this had to happen.

Monet stood up. "I've really gotta get going, gang. Eww, look at me being all alliterate and shit." This made everyone laugh, something she was good at. Being drunk didn't take much, though.

"You're in no shape to drive. Let's get you a ride," Sophie told her. She turned to me. "Or we can stay here until in the morning, right?"

"Sure," I held my arms out. "Mi casa es su casa."

"Oh, Española, I like it," Monet told me. "I'm originally from Texas, but Houston couldn't contain all this fun." She ran her index finger in a circle above her head.

"You came to Nash when you could have gone to Austin? Girl, you just lost points," Kody told her. "I visited Austin once. Never wanted to leave the place."

"I went there first and worked for a smaller recording company, but then 13 Recordings offered me a job, and it was move over Nashville, here comes trouble." Monet did a quick bow that almost ended with her face planting. Instead, it ended with us laughing our asses off.

"No, ladies, y'all are welcome to stay. There's two bedrooms."

The two silently communicated with each other and reached a decision to stay.

"Okay, we'll stay, but I'm setting my alarm. Unlike some of you, I have to work tomorrow, and I'll have to

Becks

go home to get ready. I dress rock stars, I can't go in looking all walk of shame-ish."

"I'll need to go home, too. We have to rehearse the new song in the afternoon before our show tomorrow night, Becks."

"Right. We've only done it about a thousand times." My sarcasm wasn't lost on her.

"Not in front of an audience." Her whiney speech made me smile. She never whined when she hadn't been drinking.

"I promise we'll be there with plenty of time."

She reached for me and wrapped her arms around my neck. "Thank you, Becks." She leaned into me, and I knew walking would be a problem, so I scooped her up and carried her to the extra bedroom. The others didn't follow us, so I laid her down, undressed her to her panties and bra, and tucked her in under the soft sheet and comforter.

My eyes lingered on her smooth, creamy skin. I ran my finger down her cheek as she lay with her hair fanned out across the pillow. What a picture she made. Every man's wet dream. Leaning down, I gave her a light kiss on her forehead. "Night, my sleepy Sophie girl."

When I walked out the door, Monet stood there waiting. I looked down at her. "You're sweet, Becks." She raised and kissed my cheek. "Goodnight."

"Night." She shut the door behind her.

Thia Finn

"Well, well... interesting night," Kody said picking up the girls' wine bottles and two of the four glasses they provided in my new home.

I followed him into the kitchen area. "Yeah. We've got a hell of a lot to learn about each other still."

"Pretty sure the two of you living on a fucking bus for a while will solve that problem."

"I'm sure, too." I sat at the bar beside him. He'd opened two more beers to end the night. I took a drink from the cold can. "It's going to be interesting leaving here."

He patted me on the back. "Dude, what more can you ask for? You're getting out of this damn place in search of your dream. A beautiful girl, that for my fucking life I can't wrap my head around, likes being around you enough to spend time on a bus with you. It's every musician's wish, right?"

"Yeah, I know. You're abso-fucking-lutely right. So why am I suddenly nervous about it?" I gave him a look of disbelief.

"Maybe it's because you actually feel the same about leaving with her?"

"Huh. Could be right." We finished the beer, and he crawled on my couch and snored before I had all the lights off.

Climbing in my bed, I wanted to go to sleep, but all I could think about was her in the other bedroom of my apartment. How did this happen? My life could crumble before my eyes if I wasn't careful, and if I went down, would she go with me? Was this even fair to her? So many unanswered questions crossed my mind as I tried to fall asleep.

The ding of my alarm stirred in my head. I knew I had to hit the floor running since I'd set it for the last minute. I clung to the warmth of my pillow. It smelled like perfume, fruity and floral. Maybe a little coconut. Wondering what the cleaners used on the sheets, I needed to tell them to keep using it.

I pulled the softness closer to me, and it moved on its own. *What the hell?* Opening my eyes, I realized my pillow didn't smell this good, a woman did. As I let go of her, I raised up on my elbows and knew instantly it was Sophie.

Shit, how'd she get here? I put her in her own bed.

Before my feet found the floor, she opened her eyes. "Oh, hey, Becks."

"Hey? What are you doing in my bed? I put you in the other room."

She rolled on her side and put her head in her hand. "I had to go pee in the middle of the night. Must have been all that wine. Thank God we didn't drink any beer with it this time." I gave her a direct look wanting her to get back to the story. "Yeah, and when I figured out I was in your bed instead of the one I got out of, I just stayed. Doesn't really matter. I mean, it's not like we haven't slept together in a bed before."

Raising the covers up, she glanced down. "And I'm still wearing my undies, so what's the big deal? Nothing happened, except what happened to my clothes?"

"Don't you remember?" She shook her head. Her light-hearted teasing said being undressed didn't bother her. "You decided to treat the other three of us to a little strip show after you opened that second bottle of wine." Now, I had her attention. She sat straight up, vigorously shaking her head.

"Yeah, but you know, me being the gentleman that I am, stopped you when you got down to your *undies*." I emphasized the last word to add more humor.

"Thank God. Please don't let me drink like that when we go on tour. I try to remember not to, but when I get started, I can't seem to stop myself."

I thought her reaction would be more excitable, but the story skipped over her when she excused her behavior by asking for help. The tour just got a little more exciting. I decided at some point I might warn the band going with us to keep an eye on her if she started drinking. The last thing we needed on tour was pictures of her stripping down at an after party, and I knew already Ethan lined them up for us to attend.

Chapter 21

SOPHIE

The last show turned out to be kickass. The crowd's cheers to each song told us both that our music meant something to them. The loud applause, whistles, and screaming said it all. Both of us were in awe of their reactions. We opened for Echo, and the guys fist-bumped and congratulated us as we worked our way off stage. Sophie and I flew high from it all.

"Oh. My. God. Becks, that was wild."

He picked me up and swung me around when we cleared the backstage excitement. We didn't have VIP fans behind the scenes come to see us like Echo did, but neither of us cared. The thrill from hearing the audience sing our praises said it all.

"Sure was, Sophie girl." He let my body go enough to slide down his. I could feel his excitement. My reaction must have shown all over my face because he leaned in and kissed me like his life depended on it.

At first, I feared someone would open the door and see us, but when he sucked my tongue in and deepened the kiss, I forgot all about other people. The two of us mattered more than anything else as I ran my hands up the back of his head and through the tangled hair he'd created on stage.

His hands cupped my ass, and he rocked his hard length into me. Before I could respond, we both heard voices outside the door. I jumped away from him just in time.

"Great show, you two," Ethan praised us coming through the doorway. He reached Becks first and patted him on the back, but when he looked up at me, his smile faded. I knew my swollen lips told him what he didn't want to know, but it was too late. Becks might not care as he'd plainly told me before, but I did.

Before he spoke, the door opened again, and the guys from the band entered. While our scene might have been tense, it ended as soon as the three walked in talking and laughing.

"That show was legit, people." They stuck their hands up to high five everyone else. It made me happy because these guys had given me hell during the early practices, but now I knew why. They made me better, more confident. Best of all, they were willing to give me a chance to show them what I could do. They never talked down to me or belittled me, but they wouldn't hold back on calling me on my shit when I tried to give up.

Once the guys found the ice chest full of beer, all their compliments ended, and Ethan got back to us. "So, uh... I wanted to tell you both before the clowns arrived how ridiculous the show was. The fans' insanity kept the noise going the whole time. That's what the label wants to see the entire time you're on tour."

"Thanks, Ethan. We want that, too." Becks acted as though nothing happened before the band stopped Ethan.

"I have to ask..." He looked between the two of us, and I knew what he was about to say. The answer Becks gave him would determine what I said.

"Yeah, what's that?" Becks didn't let it go.

"Is this..." he waved his finger between Becks and me, "... going to be a problem?"

Becks said, "No," immediately, so Ethan turned to me and raised an eyebrow.

"No, I mean. I don't see that it will." My face heated up, and I knew the blush started at my neck and worked its way up.

Becks wrapped his arm around behind my waist. "We're both consenting adults, Ethan, and we both want what's best for our careers. Right now, being together is best for us both. Who knows where it'll go, but either way, we'll handle it. Right, Sophie?"

"Right. We didn't plan on anything happening between us. It just did. And it can stop just as quickly if we decide on it. Nothing will stop us from achieving what we set out to do." I knew I sounded more convinced than I felt, but for now, I needed it to.

"Okay, I'll hold you both to it. You might want to consider if you're ready for this to be public, though, because once the fans get a hold of it, who knows what kind of response you'll get. The females will be jealous, that much I can assure you of. They are far more aggressive than male fans, so be prepared to deal with negative comments, Sophie."

I nodded at him. "Yeah, such is the life of a pretty rock star."

Becks laughed. "Not a star without you, Sophie girl. We're a team."

"Tell her that when those crazies try to rip your clothes off while ignoring her. You know you'll also have women propositioning him directly in front of you, too."

"I think she can handle them. You should see her have a bitch fit. Scares the shit out of me." Both men laughed.

"He's trying to say that I can defend him when I need to, and I'm not afraid to step up and do it. Just because his muscles stand out for everyone to see doesn't mean the rest of us don't know how to take care of ourselves."

Ethan looked hard at me and then smiled. "Yeah, I bet you can."

"Four boys lived next door to me. If I planned to live past my tenth birthday, I had to learn to fight for myself."

Both men laughed again before Ethan spoke. "Sounds like she's the one you want around in a beatdown, Becks."

"Hell yeah. My girl's a spitfire."

We all laughed, and Becks kissed the side of my head.

Guess the secret was out now, at least in front of the band and our manager.

Cold air blasted as we stepped on the tour bus. "Holy shit. Look at this huge fucker. We're going to be ritzy for a few months." Sophie rubbed her palm across the grained leather of the chair closest to the entrance of the living area.

"Yeah, wonder who's gonna be sharing with us? I mean, surely this isn't just for the two of us." He dropped my guitar case and flung his entire body down the entire length of the extra-long couch."

The door reopened, and we both heard a voice we recognized, Monet.

"Squeee!" The deafening sound we made had Becks holding his ears. Monet and I jumped up and down in the center aisle, going around and around.

"This is going to be the best road trip, *ever*," I emphasized the word even louder.

"I know, right. When Ethan called last night and told me he wanted me on the bus, I jumped at the chance."

I turned to Becks, and the look he gave me didn't say 'kick-ass road trip.'

Monet saw the same thing. "Awe Becks, what's the matter, sweetie?" she asked in a too sweet, shrill voice. "Afraid I'm going to be the cock-blocker for the next few months?"

He said nothing just stood and looked between the two of us, then stomped down the hallway.

Turning back to Monet, I barked laughter. "Poor guy. He's so mistreated. *Not.* Don't worry, he'll get over it."

She raised the volume of her voice. "Especially when I tell him how into threesomes I am, and this will be the best months of his life."

Stomping came back toward us. "Threesomes? Are you for real or just shitting me?"

A sly smile grew across her face. "Guess we'll have to consult your squeeze here."

Becks

"Bitch, I'm no one's squeeze, unless I'm the new and only squeeze," I told them both.

"Damn, you two are too easy. Just remember that when I sneak my own flavor on here for some rock and roll time." Her hips thrust forward, and we all started laughing. I knew this trip had so many possibilities, but they grew exponentially when Monet climbed on board.

We finished the grand tour to find bunks on each side, an extra small bath with a shower, and finally an area in the back that looked like pit seating minus the fireplace. We stored our things, found places for guitars and the equipment Monet brought. She would serve as our makeup, clothing, and general flunky.

"Hey, Sophie, Becks?" a voice called from the front.

I moved out of my bunk finding Ethan and another man standing there. "Oh, hey," I greeted them.

Becks and Monet came forward standing behind me.

"This is Jonathan. He'll be driving this beast. He's top notch at what he does. Can park this thing anywhere we need it."

I raised my hand and gave the huge man a wave. He looked like a beast himself. Becks stepped forward and shook the older man's hand.

Monet grinned. "Hello, Mr. Mastadon. I'm sorry, but dude, you don't even look like a Jonathan to me."

He laughed. "I've been called a helluva lot worse."

Thia Finn

"Oh, that wasn't meant as a negative thing. You're just a fucking big ol' guy, but I'm sure you've heard that, too."

He nodded. "I don't let much bother me, but so you'll know, I'm more of a gentle giant than a massive elephant with tusks."

"Noted, dude. Honestly, I know who I'll scream for if I'm ever in trouble." Monet sidled up beside him and wrapped his bicep in her palm. Her small hand didn't come close to reaching around it. "See, this right here is exactly what I'm talking about."

Jonathan grinned down at her, and from the look on his face, I knew she'd won him over. He might be a giant, but he was her new puppy.

"Okay," Ethan spoke again. "You're going to be leaving this afternoon for St. Louis, then down to Memphis, Little Rock, Tallahassee, Birmingham, Atlanta, Charlotte, Huntington, Cincinnati, Columbus, Indianapolis, Lexington, Knoxville, and back to Nash. You'll have some time off to regroup and do studio work before we send you out again."

"Damn. How long will that take?" I asked the question we all wondered about.

"Three weeks. You'll be playing four shows each week, plus you'll be doing radio shows at the ass crack of dawn. You'll also have downtime to do some writing together."

We talked about doing some co-writing but hadn't had time to make it happen. Guess being stuck on a

Page | **208**

Becks

bus for three weeks, we might if we weren't dead tired. Looking at Becks, he nodded and smiled as though he knew exactly what played across my mind.

"When you get back, I expect some music you're ready to show the band, so we can get tracks laid prior to leaving again. Striking while you're hot. It's important. We get your tunes out on the radio, the shows get your faces out there. We'll be building a fan base on social media."

Ethan's speech turned into a laundry list for us. Play shows, write music, radio appearances, update social media as much as possible. *Would sleep be scheduled for us too?*

"Your next time out, we'll be sending you west to Cali, then north to Portland, Seattle, and more."

"Wow, Ethan. This is all happening at light speed," I told him as I sat down at the small dining table. "I never realized how fast it would explode."

Becks stooped down beside me. "Is there a problem, Sophie girl? Isn't this what you wanted?"

My palm touched his beautiful face. "You know it is. It's falling into place like a dream. I'm trying to wrap my head around it, is all. I'm thrilled beyond belief over everything."

"Good," Ethan cut in moving to the front of the bus. "So, your first show's tomorrow night. Be ready."

We all said our goodbyes, and Jonathan stepped into his area of the bus sitting down in his driver's seat. The motor roared to life, and he eased the beast into traffic from the warehouse where we gathered.

Today, our lives changed forever. My heart skipped a beat when I thought of it. I glanced at Becks and smiled. He gave me a big one back before leaning forward and kissing me.

"You ready, Sophie girl?"

"Hell, yeah. You?" I threw my hands up in the air in excitement.

"Abso-fucking-lutely." Becks' hands joined mine.

Monet opened a single-serve wine bottle. "I'll drink to that." She raised her free hand.

Chapter 22

BECKS

The Ready Room in St. Louis welcomed us when we walked in the evening we arrived. We looked around to see how the venue was set up. I fucking loved playing in small venues like this because watching the people made a lot of difference in our performance. After this tour, Ethan promised we would be opening for a big band, and I knew the locations would be a lot larger.

"Well, what do you think?" I glanced at Sophie as she took in the crowd hanging out in front of the stage waiting for the first set of the night.

She backed over to me, and I wrapped my arms around her from behind molding her body to mine. That floral, fruity scent went straight to my dick. Something about it called to my basic instincts and made me want to scoop her up and take her somewhere more private. Sometimes I thought I smelled some almond too. Damn, all those together could cause me to do nasty things to her in public.

"I think it's the perfect size for us to start. Do you think they'll all be this small?"

"No, but I doubt they'll be much larger. We need to get our feet wet before we swim across the ocean, Sophie girl." I kissed her ear after speaking softly into it. Running my tongue down behind her ear, her body gave an involuntary shiver. I knew what to do to keep her mind on me.

"Stop. How am I supposed to be thinking when you're doing that?"

"What? Oh, you mean this?" Again, I moved my tongue by her ear, but this time, I ran it up the outer edge as I watched goosebumps trail down her arm.

"Exactly." She didn't want me to stop, or she had a strange way of showing it since she leaned back on my shoulder and wrapped her arms over mine. Sitting on the barstool, I kept her pulled tightly to me. I knew she could feel my dick growing behind her with no space between us.

Monet sat next to me but seemed unaware of our constant foreplay going on. "So, Monet, what do you think?" I looked over at her.

"I think the two of you need to stop giving a show or the crowd will be watching you instead of the band."

Sophie and I both started laughing. "I promise to be good," Sophie told her. "But what Becks does is a different story. It's all on him."

"That's right, Soph, I want you all on me."

She turned her head, and those hazel eyes met mine, desire written in them.

"Stop it, you two, or I *will* find a stranger to bring home on the bus. I'm not above a one-night stand, especially since I can kick them out in the morning."

"Them? You plan to bring more than one home?" Watching might have just become my newest pleasure.

"My meaning was more as in male or female, but a threesome is never out of the question."

Sophie and I both sat staring at her speechless. I honestly didn't have a comeback to her announcement. Not that I cared what she did or who she did it with, to each his own, but I wouldn't have guessed she played both sides of the coin.

"Ha. Shocked y'all, didn't I?" Sophie nodded her head. "I'm not picky is the thing when it comes to sex. I like it all."

"Oh, yeah? That's good to know. I won't be surprised now when I wake up in the morning on the bus to three women instead of two."

"Or it could be one of each. Like I said, I like it all and sometimes, if I'm feeling it, the more the merrier. You know?"

Thia Finn

"Well, your space is limited so don't get too carried away on your invitations."

"Right. I considered that when I looked at the general sleeping arrangements. Did y'all know the back area converts to a huge bed?" She winked at us just before the lights went down, and the first sticks clacked together from the drummer.

This tour just got a lot more interesting. Big beds, multiple partners, and a wild woman on board. Damn, it made me harder thinking about it.

The band we watched played a set of loud hard rock. I enjoyed it, but Sophie didn't seem too impressed. "I'm ready to go if y'all are," she told us gathering her purse closer to her as if she planned to leave quickly.

Monet and I both nodded since hearing over the crowd noise became impossible as soon as the band walked off stage. We ventured out to the street and walked down to the next location. A band played but not the loud rock we had been treated to before.

We listened to a set of alternative rock and agreed the sound hit closer to home for us.

"I'm ready to go back to the bus," Monet announced outside of the club. "It's been a long day for me, and I have plans for tomorrow to meet up with some friends kinda early."

"Sounds good to me, too." What I really wanted to do was have Sophie on the bus. After all the grinding that took place in the dark of the club, if she touched me just right, I might embarrass myself like a fourteen-year-old on his first date.

The Uber driver took us straight to the door of the parked bus. Jonathan had his own area behind the driver's seat where he slept and watched television. We punched in the code and opened the door to a soft glow and a loud snore which made us all quietly laugh. He obviously could sleep through anything since we didn't hear any movement, and the loud snorts never let up.

Monet looked at us. "See you guys in the morning. Wrap it before you tap it." She climbed into her bunk and pulled the curtain closed.

"Very funny, Monet," Sophie told her. "We'll be sure to make extra loud noises for you to get off on." No reply came. "Guess she wears earplugs to bed."

"I hope she does, noise-canceling ones because I plan on making you scream my name more than once tonight."

"On that little bunk?"

"Actually, I thought we might investigate that bed she talked about." I moved to the back of the bus, past the bath area and opened the folding door. The flimsiness provided privacy only. So much for keeping down the noises. It only took a few minutes to figure out how to convert it to a king-size bed. Thank God. Doing the deed in the bunk would give new meaning to boundaries.

I walked back to the front, and Sophie stood there in only her panties and bra. "What the fuck, Sophie girl? Jonathan might've come in here."

"His snoring never stopped. I doubt he's awake again before morning. Besides..." her hands found the bottom of my t-shirt, "... I wanted to surprise you, and the last time you had me dressed this way, I slept under the covers beside you. Remember?"

Her fingernails scraped over my abs causing my muscles to contract, defining each section of my six pack, as she took the shirt up my body. Before she reached my pecs, I grabbed it behind my head and pulled straight up, removing it. If she wanted to explore, I granted her better access.

She leaned in and kissed across my chest from one nipple to the other before circling her tongue around the flat nub. The warm wetness caused them to stand out before she licked the rough flat surface across one. God, it felt amazing.

Pushing me backward down the aisle, she unfolded the door and latched it behind her. I stood still in the small space waiting to see where this was going. When she turned around, she started where she left off and her pointed tongue traced the lines of my abdomen. I needed to touch her but held back allowing her to continue the way she wanted.

She went down on her knees in front of me and unbuttoned my jeans. Before touching the zipper that restrained my swollen cock, she looked up at me as if

Becks

asking for permission. Like she needed my permission. Hell, I'd help her get the damn jeans off if she'd let me. I liked where this was going, and right then, I needed it to move to at hyper speed.

"Please, Soph." I could beg when necessary.

A soft smile appeared on her beautiful lips as she moved the zipper down, one tooth at a time. At least, it seemed that way to me. She pulled my jeans down from the waistband on each side of me, taking my underwear with it. I swear the girl moved in slow motion. The movement tortured me in the best way.

My dick bobbed out, but with the rock hardness, it popped up almost hitting my stomach. To add to the torture, she didn't start with it but wrapped my balls in her warm palm, lightly fondling them as she moved forward and took one nut in her mouth.

"Oh God. Yes, Soph, that's going to kill me." I ran my hand down the back of her head, fingering the smooth hair. I thought about wrapping it around my hand and helping her get on with her exploration but decided against it. This was all on her.

Her palms started at my knees and slowly caressed their way upward as she took the other ball in her mouth. Before she reached the tops of my legs, she left my balls and put her tongue at the base of my cock, running the flattened warmth up to the head. Her hands cupped both balls and assaulted them in the softest way before she ran one finger around the seam to behind the boys and lightly grazed my anus. It caused me to go to war with my brain to keep from busting a nut all over us both. Damn this woman.

I reached under her arms and pulled her up then pushed her on the bed. "You're killing me. I can't wait any longer to touch you."

"Touch me, Becks. Touch me everywhere."

She didn't have to ask.

NEWS REPORT EIGHT

Anchor: Breaking news from the Channel 8 Newsroom. We've just learned that an arrest warrant has been issued in the death of Judge and Mrs. Beckon Masters. For more on this, we turn to Janna Alfred with the latest. Janna?

Janna: Yes, thank you, Lisa. I'm here at the Lawback County Courthouse where we've just learned that an arrest warrant has been issued in the death of the Judge and his wife, Mrs. Masters. As you might recall, a devastating fire occurred at their home about ten miles from here. The warrants issued were for the couple's two sons in connection with their death. These two have not come forward with information nor have their whereabouts been discovered. Stay tuned for more information in this unfolding situation here on *Channel 8 NEWS*.

Anchor: Thank you, Janna. As you might recall, the Judge and his wife's bodies were found in the burned-out remains of their home. Arson investigators claim the fire was started from a burning cigar, but accelerants were also found around the home. The Masters' home was gutted by the fire, and their bodies were found on the second floor. At the time, a clear determination of this case being labeled as arson had not been decided.

Judge Masters served as a county judge who presided over many high-profile cases in the county until his retirement from the bench because of medical issues. He was said to be a stern judge during his tenure often giving maximum sentences to those who he felt set examples for others.

BECKS

Dreaming of sharing a bus with two females had living hell written all over it, but the three of us worked out well. We slept in while the bus rolled down the road and got up in a new city almost every damn day. Sophie and I prepared for the next show while Monet tripped over what we would wear and how we would look on stage, something I gave zero fucks about.

We wrote together on our few off days off. Sleeping together created new feelings, and the words and music flowed between us. I felt a closeness to Sophie I'd never had before with a woman. Growing up, I didn't have girlfriends, even in high school. I chilled with my brother and his friends mostly. Maybe my laziness or disinterest in people hanging around all the time kept them away. I preferred practicing my guitar and keyboard over people.

Sophie must have spent a lot of time with her music too because her guitar skills matched mine. She never took the time to learn the piano, though. That needed to change in my opinion. Playing more than one instrument always provided a more diverse sound.

She still suffered some on the stage performance but nothing like in the beginning. When her nerves weren't on high alert, she performed like a champ. I needed to figure out a way to get her that loose on the stage all the time.

The news about us spread like wildfire, and our fans—yes, we had fans now—started following us both in person and on all the social media. Whenever we had a show, Twitter would blow up with accolades we dreamed of. It dominoed, thanks to the mad skills some of the supporters had with Snapchat and the others. They also posted what city we played in next.

Videos would show up as live online. Short clips they posted had us tagged so we could see them and the comments and reposts. We fucking loved it. Just thinking about what these people did to get the word out made us crazy.

The shows started selling out. What more could we ask for?

Ethan messaged us to express his praise and how damn angry he was at himself for allowing us to play

Becks

in some of the smaller venues. He knew now we could step up to the next level, but Sophie and I played for excited crowds, and fucking loved every minute of it. The closeness we shared with an audience seemed surreal at times. Hell, getting to see and hear them sing our songs proved to be a high no drug could ever provide.

The Columbus skyline stood out against the early morning colors of blue and pink. The bus sat parked in a lot closer to the venue. We all needed a day off. The touring life upheld all the shit we had been told to expect, but constantly moving down the road got old. The label sprung for a hotel room for the one night we could check into in the afternoon. We jumped at the opportunity. I wished for a real bathroom, something I never thought I would do.

Monet's friends waited for the bus to stop and then whisked her away for the remainder of the day and night. With our show not until the second night, we had some time to do what we damn well pleased for a change. Ethan scheduled a radio interview for the following morning, and we're supposed to play a few songs live, something we had yet to do.

When our bus mate drove off, I turned and gave Sophie my deviously best 'I know what we can do now' look.

"Oh please, you're so predictable. Such a man."

Thia Finn

"Sophie girl, I've got your man right here waiting." I grabbed my junk and shook it. She laughed out loud. If I had a fragile ego, she crushed it.

"What's going on back there?" Jonathan questioned from his area.

"Shhh. Now you've woken up the third party."

"No, she didn't. This third wheel is leaving. I've got some things to do, and then I'll check into my room. Maybe I'll see y'all tonight there. I'm not coming back here." The bus door closed with a whoosh.

"You think that was his way of telling us we have the whole bus to ourselves for an unlimited time?" Sophie looked at me.

I nodded. "Alone time. What will we do with ourselves?" I wiggled my eyebrows.

"Oh, you know. Sleep some more. Eat some lunch. Chill. Whatever." Her innocuous answer made me want to laugh. Instead, I slowly moved toward her.

"There's a thousand things that fall under whatever, Sophie girl. I plan to do at least half of those things to you before we see anyone again." I looked out the small window over the sink. "Everyone who knows we're here thinks we've gone somewhere already. So no interruptions."

"You mean, just you and me and this whole big bus?" She gestured around her.

I glanced behind and in front of me, visualizing all the surfaces I could take her. My dick grew harder behind my zipper the more places I saw in my mind.

Becks

Tabletop, couch, fridge, wall, doors. Unlimited places waiting to be christened.

As I stepped forward, she stepped back and pulled her soft t-shirt over her head. Her beautiful breasts stood at attention begging for me.

"Your turn." The soft words passed her lips. I quickly indulged her, throwing my shirt with hers. I captured her before she could take another step away, wrapping my arms around hers pinning them to her sides. I slid my chest down hers, dragging against her soft skin. Damn, it felt like heaven with those taut nipples scraping along my pecs.

When I reached my knees, I had her hands trapped beside her hips. She watched me admire her rosy tips as I kissed across her stomach moving upward toward them. My nose nudged the underside of each as I nipped over the velvety skin below each before I captured one pebble and then the other.

Sophie sucked in a deep breath when I finally seized the spot she needed lavished. I ran my tongue around the pink and then pulled the nub with my teeth gripping just enough to sting.

"Oh God, Becks. That feels amazing." My hands moved down to her legs beneath the loose sleep shorts. Her fingers ran through my hair to my scalp, scraping my head with her nails. I imagined my teeth on her equaled her nails on me. Slight pain, a lot of pleasure.

I continued slowly down her silky thighs, happy Monet insisted on her getting waxed, the smoothness undeniable. Leaving the hardened nipples behind, I kissed above her waistband and then over the shorts until I reached the lips that concealed what I searched for. I bit softly at the mound before taking a deep breath knowing her craving matched mine.

"Sophie..." The begging tone in my voice said everything. "Let's take these off." Her thumbs hooked in the band, but I stopped her. "Let me." I pulled from the legs knowing the elastic would slide easily over her hips. A sparse piece of lace allowed a vision of perfectly bare skin. Again, I bit the mound hiding what I wanted. This time, I tasted her desire as I ran my tongue up the fine lace.

I tugged the lace down with my lips enough to see the swollen flesh peeking at me begging for more. Taking the thin elastic with my fingers, I took it to the floor, and she stepped out. Heaven exposed itself right in front of my eyes. Taking her right leg over my shoulder, I leaned in and licked her from back to front capturing her pink clit. My tongue circled the stiff point causing her to moan louder.

She spread her legs wider on my shoulder begging for more attention. I skimmed my hand lightly up her thigh to the apex slick with her arousal. While my tongue continued to assault her, two fingers pushed inside her. Her muscles clamped down on them intending to hold them in place, but they had other ideas as they pumped in and out of the tight passage.

When I added a third finger, she felt the snugness and bucked forward giving me better access to the spot I knew she needed. I crooked one finger forward in search of the roughness that was bound to set off a hard orgasm. Rubbing across it as I lightly bit her nub on the outside caused her leg muscles to tighten, her back to arch. Hell, maybe even her toes to curl. Her body seized in an uncontrolled tremor over and over, and I worked her over in every way.

Sophie finally opened her eyes looking down at me. I pulled my fingers out and sucked them into my mouth.

She moaned. "You're going to kill me, Becks."

"Oh, babe. Killing you isn't on the list of things I'm going to do to you now we're truly alone."

I stood and reached under her thighs wrapping her legs around my waist. Sophie's hands traced a path on my neck, lightly scraping her nails across it, before they clasped together. She followed her nails with the point of her tongue tracing the marks she left. A chill ran down my arm from her touch causing me to speed things up. I turned and backed her into the solid wall grinding my rock-hard cock into her exactly where my grinding would do the most for her.

We made our way to the real bed waiting to be broken in by the two of us.

Chapter 24

BECKS

We woke the next morning tired from the night of pure enjoyable pleasure. Our time ended with both our phone alarms going off. "Guess our alone time is done for now."

"Yeah but we still have tonight in the hotel room we didn't make it to last night."

"We could go there to shower and dress." I looked at the clock.

An easy, hot smile graced her lips. "Or we could stay here and go one more round."

Becks

Talking to only a couple of people in a crowded booth allowed us to be ourselves. Sophie quickly forgot about the microphones sending out our conversation to thousands of listeners in radioland. I fucking loved watching her with the DJ. She flirted and played him at every turn. This girl charmed the guy like nothing I'd ever seen. Once she broke out of the shyness shell, she shined for all to see.

I sat back and watched her. She didn't perform, it was all-natural laughter and fun banter between the two. This woman grew with every new opportunity presented. Between her music and this, I knew great things were damn sure going to be happening. I hoped I would always be around to see it.

"What do you want to do now?" I questioned her as we walked out to the waiting cab.

"I don't care. Have you ever been here before?"

"No. You?"

"No. Let's Google what there's to do in Columbus." She had her phone out looking online.

"Or we could go back to the bus." My idea sounded a whole lot better than sightseeing.

"Becks..." Her face was hilarious, it wasn't exactly a pout but close to it. "We have a show tonight. Besides if we're going to travel, we need to see where we're going. This is it." She showed me the phone screen with people riding on Segways.

"The fuck? We'll kill ourselves on those especially in traffic, Sophie."

"No, we won't. They look fun to me. We need to do this."

"And who'll do the show tonight if one of us gets hurt." I stared at her because the girl could be uncoordinated at times. If either of us got hurt, the label would be pissed.

"We're not getting hurt. Come on, they have another tour starting in an hour, and it includes lunch. Let's do it." Her enthusiasm resembled a little kid wanting a new toy, so I couldn't deny her. This girl wrapped me tighter each day. I knew the band would soon be asking what pocket of her purse my balls hid out in.

"Okay, but then back to the bus so we can prepare for the show?"

"Is that what you're calling it now? Good cover. No one will ever guess." She laughed and directed the driver to the new address.

They required a short lesson on riding the two-wheeled thing. It only took about a minute, and I was fucking addicted. I would have one of my own. I don't know when I'd ride it, but I felt like we could put it in storage under the bus.

Driving it behind a guide, not so fun. He made us go slow and never gave us a chance to haul ass and kick up dust. Didn't matter, though. When I had my own, I could do whatever I wanted.

Becks

I yelled at Sophie, "I'm so glad we did this. I fucking love it." She grinned at me and rolled forward on her feet taking off behind the guide.

We played over an hour stopping to look at things before he stopped us at an outdoor café. The two of us ate and drank the one beer we were given.

"This is a great way to spend our day, Becks. You know, doing things we both enjoy."

I watched her continue to pick at her chips. Sophie was more than just a beautiful woman. Sure she could sing and play the guitar, but she also liked to do fun things. She rarely turned down an opportunity to go somewhere or try out something new. Watching her live made me want more with her. More time. More everything.

The rest of our shows took us back to Nashville since we had passed the halfway mark in the tour dates. Ethan planned our every minute for what seemed like the next year. It made me happy to think I'd be sharing it with Sophie.

"What are you thinking about? You're a million miles away."

"Oh, I was thinking about the tour being halfway over already."

"Yeah, I'm glad and sad at the same time."

"I know what you mean." I knew exactly what she meant.

"Do you?" I waited to see how she would answer.

Thia Finn

"I'm ready to get off the road a while, but it won't be the same without being with you every day. And Monet either."

"Monet? Oh, right." Maybe she'd miss us the same.

"We're with her every day, Becks. I really like her. She's fun and thoughtful, and she makes us laugh."

"Right. I know, but I thought more about the two of us not being together more." I leaned in and lightly kissed her pink lips. "It's gonna suck, you not living where I live."

"I know, but we'll still see each other every day."

"That's not going to be the same. I'm going to fucking hate it, Sophie girl. I like you with me. It's where you belong."

"Is that right? Well, I'll tell you a little secret... I like being with you, too." She peered at me through her lashes. "The truth is, I just like you... a lot, Becks."

I kissed her again, this time with more intensity. I pulled her from her seat and into my lap to deepen the kiss. We finally broke apart, and she leaned her forehead on mine. "Good. We're on the same page then."

Someone cleared their throat, obviously to gain our attention. I held Sophie close and looked over my shoulder where our guide stood.

"Is there a problem, dude?" I asked.

"We need y'all to keep it PG here in the restaurant, please." He glanced around, and my eyes followed his.

Page | **232**

Becks

People stared at us like they'd never seen a kiss. I grinned and waved at them.

"Just a kiss, guys. Sorry if we disturbed your lunch." Turning back to Sophie, she giggled, and it was the sweetest sound I had heard all day. She stood and pulled me to my feet.

"Let's go back to our toy."

"Good idea."

The entire ride back to the hotel, I thought about what Sophie and I said to each other. Hell, I didn't come to Nashville looking for anything other than the attention of a label. A lot of shit followed me around, and the last thing I wanted was getting involved with a woman.

Something about this girl kept drawing me in, though. Spending time with her made me happy. It wasn't just our music that captured my attention.

Anything other than music rarely made me happy these days. We laughed and joked around. Sophie was smart and beautiful, but she was more than those two things. Her kindness and easy-going attitude made spending time with her simple and uncomplicated. I could relax and enjoy myself for a change.

I reached for her hand and pulled it into my lap, smiling at her. She returned the look. Her eyes today held a lighter green color. The brown flecks seem to shoot across her irises. Something in my heart took a new beat.

Thia Finn

I looked straight ahead. *What the hell was that?* She said she liked me too, but did this have what it took to be more than like at some point? Thinking about further down the road left me feeling perplexed. If we continued on this path, could we make it last? The music business didn't always make for lasting relationships.

"You sure seem to be deep in thought, Becks." She looked at me. "Are you okay?"

"Yeah, I'm great. Just thinking about our show tonight. Playing the new music, you know. It's your song. I want it to be perfect."

"Me, too. Can you imagine what a disaster it would be if we screwed it up on stage?"

"We won't screw it up, Sophie girl. How many times did we rehearse this with the band? We've yet to fuck up a single song since we started playing together. Tonight, we won't either."

"I know, but there's always a first time."

"Think positive thoughts."

"Is that what you were doing when you seemed lost just now?" She watched me as though she tried to judge my answer. No way could she ever guess what I considered when she broke into my thoughts.

"I wasn't lost. I ran the riff I play at the beginning. Don't you do that?" I removed my hand from hers and played the notes on my air guitar recreating the sounds with my mouth.

Becks

"Play air guitar?" She laughed at my rendition of the song. "Hell yeah. I'm a master at air guitar, but it's better when I can stand up and add stage movements." She began playing her own while I mouthed the tunes we made.

The driver pulled up to the hotel entrance and looked over his shoulder at us. "I might have to come see that set if it sounds like that. I'd say you both are talented at air guitar." The three of us laughed as I paid the guy. "Thanks, dude."

Keys waited for us at the desk, so we went up to our rooms. Sophie and Monet's room attached to mine, but it wasn't necessary. Beside me was the only place in a bed Sophie would be keeping warm. Our bags sat in the rooms already.

She walked around the bed and looked out the window. "Hey, look at the awesome view they gave us." She stepped back pulling the curtain aside, and another building blocked everything.

I wrapped her in my arms from behind. "All the view I need is in this room."

She looked over her shoulder and rolled her eyes. "Cheesy much?"

I spun her around to face me. I wanted to see her reactions as I spoke. "It's true. I don't need a view of downtown when the most beautiful woman in it stands in front of me."

Thia Finn

"Becks. Are you trying to get me in a real bed?" A sexy-as-hell smile crossed her lips. She thought this was about sex.

"No, I'm trying to tell you that I might have lied in the taxi." Her eyebrow shot up.

"A little white lie. I needed to stall for time," I confessed to her. Lying wasn't something I did, but at this point, a huge omission hung between us. That piece of information needed to wait for another time or maybe never.

"You're making no sense at all, Becks." She ran her hands across my shoulders and up to the back of my neck, linking them together.

"When we talked to each other at the café about how much I liked you, I kept playing that over and over in my mind on our way back and then again in the taxi."

Her eyes searched my face. Did she wonder where this was going? I picked my words carefully.

"And?" Her one word nudged me forward.

"I meant what I said, Sophie. I haven't been in a real relationship, ever."

Her voice raised a full octave. "Ever?"

My head shook. "High school was... complicated. Other than my brother, I stayed to myself most of the time. My guitar held my interest, but that was it. I taught myself the keyboard, too."

She raised an eyebrow in questions. "You can learn anything from YouTube if you watch it enough. I ate up all the data on my phone. Made the old bastard mad as hell about it, too."

"I'm assuming you're talking about your father."

"Yeah." Talking about him was off limits today. "Anyway, the girls in my school weren't into music, at least none I found. Maybe I didn't look for any either."

"I find it hard to believe they didn't come looking for you." She tugged on my hair. "Did you have all this hair back then?"

"In my last year, I started growing it out mostly to piss off my dad. I just stopped getting it cut. Anyway, what I'm trying to say is, I feel things for you that I'm new at. I see you as this wonderful, gorgeous woman who stands on the edge of greatness. Being beside you in this makes me see that it could happen. To be honest, though, I want more than that with you."

"Oh, Becks. If you're trying to melt my heart, you've succeeded."

"We don't know where our lives will take us yet, but I feel like if we're together, it doesn't matter. I'm not sure I'm in love or anything because hell, I've never even been in like before, so love is a shooting star at this point."

She reached up and softly kissed me. Her forehead leaned into mine. I felt her breath hitch. "That's a beautiful thing to say."

"Yeah, so I guess where I'm trying to go with this is... I hope you feel something this strong for me, too. Or maybe, you're still thinking if it could possibly happen, which I'm okay with, too. Are you willing to give us a chance? You know, to see where it might go?"

As I leaned into her, my nose lightly touched hers on one side. I nuzzled across it, our lips so close but not touching. She said, "Yes," so softly I barely heard the response.

Was she afraid to commit to it?

Did this scare her like it did me because, at that moment, I quaked in my chucks.

Pulling her closer to me, I claimed her lips. The kiss branded her to me. For good or bad, our connection sealed with the smoldering, wet kiss and an intensity that burned straight into my heart.

BECKS

We ran on stage, and the drummer pounded his sticks counting out the beat. The crowd went wild for us as we began the first song of our set. SoBeck played several songs before we stopped and Sophie spoke to the crowd. Her bravery for speaking increased with each show. My pride showed when I smiled as she introduced us. I wanted my girl to be able to do what she was meant to do, entertain.

"How are you tonight, Columbus?" she yelled into the microphone setting off a loud roaring noise. "We are SoBeck, and we're happy to be in your city. Today we explored it some and found lots of fun things to do. We especially loved the old parts of downtown. How about the whole German Village area?"

Thia Finn

The crowd again responded, and we took that as our cue to start the next few songs. We saw the people in the front singing along to our music, something I doubted I'd ever get used to. Realizing people knew our songs that well was amazing.

The set wound down, and we played one of our new ones before ending the night with Sophie's song included on the EP that Ethan sent to all the radio DJs. The crowd loved it when she introduced it as her song. She'd gained their trust with each song tonight, and this one capped it off.

"Direct Attention" came from a time when she played the cover songs at the bars. The words told of how lonely it made her when she sang the words of others when she wanted the audience to hear her words instead. The crowd loved it to the point that I thought she might cry. She had to turn and face the band to get it together.

We finished out with "Beyond the Words." The people kept the applause going while our equipment was torn down and removed so the headliners could perform. If we were the headliners, we would be doing a couple more songs for an encore, but that option wasn't given to us.

Monet, Sophie, and I started out the back of the venue and to the bus since we would be leaving as soon as everything was set to go. Only three more shows until we rolled back into Nashville.

Who knew what our lives would be like when we got there.

SOPHIE

"Oh God, I'm beat. Maybe we should've come back and taken a nap after our ride."

"What did y'all do? I made it back to my room just in time to get your clothes for tonight. Good thing I'd already picked out what you needed," Monet told us as we walked through double doors into a hallway. She'd talked the entire time we dressed about the fun she had with her friends.

I turned at looked at Becks raising one eyebrow. What would we say? Fucked? Made love? Had sex? Before I chose a euphemism to try out, Becks spoke up, "We did what any couple would do that had some extra time on their hands in a hotel room." He smiled to himself causing Monet to laugh. I felt the heat rising up. I didn't really care that she knew what we did, but the way he said it made us sound so normal. Our sex was never normal.

Becks opened the doors to the back parking lot where the bus motor roared, ready to leave. Red flashing lights glared around the edges of the bus.

"I wonder if someone tried to break into the busses during the show?"

"Surely they wouldn't be that fucking stupid. The drivers are usually on them and Jonathan carries a pistol," Becks informed us of information we didn't know. I supposed in his position, carrying made sense.

We continued to our bus where several police officers stood outside the door talking to Jonathan and the driver from the band's bus.

One policeman stepped forward in front of Becks. "Are you Becks O'Donnell Masters?"

That was strange. I'd never heard the name Masters attached to his. Becks O'Donnell is all he ever called himself.

"Yes, sir. I am."

"Mr. Masters, there's a warrant for your arrest in Tennessee for arson and murder."

"What?" I yelled. "There's no way Becks killed someone. Right, Becks?"

"No, Sophie. This is not true," he said it so calmly that I couldn't help but stare at him. If it were me, I'd be freaking out. Becks stood there and took it like it was not a problem for him. Being arrested at all was bad, but for murder, this was huge.

Becks

I backed away, and Monet wrapped her arm around my shoulders. "How could this be, Monet? He's been with us."

The officer read his Miranda rights as he handcuffed him.

Becks kept his eyes on me the entire time. "Call Ethan, Sophie, since this might be our last show."

The officer pushed his head through the backseat car door and shut it. Becks looked out the window at me. I thought his lips said 'I love you' but couldn't tell for sure.

I needed to think. We needed a plan. What I needed was Becks.

My mind couldn't comprehend the scene.

I felt Monet's arm around my shoulders.

"What are we going to do, Monet? What will happen to him? What will happen to us?"

Silence answered.

NEWS REPORT NINE

Reporter: You've just witnessed the arrest warrant being served and the apprehension of one of the suspects in the arson and murder investigation of Judge and Mrs. Beckon Masters. One son, Becks O'Donnell Masters, has been taken into custody in conjunction with this heinous crime committed on his parents.

O'Donnell Masters will be taken to the County Courthouse here in Columbus where he will remain pending the extradition from Ohio to Tennessee taking place. Stay tuned as we follow this story. Janna Alfred, reporting for *Channel 8 NEWS*.

Book Two of *Becks* coming soon

All hell breaks loose when the team rolls back into Nashville to find Becks.

The fire that killed his parents uncovers secrets better left in the ashes of the burned-out home.

Konan, Beck's brother, also adds to the confusion and tales from their childhood.

While Sophie's music moves back to Nashville bars, Becks' songs are written in the worst of conditions—a jail cell.

Will their budding relationship survive?

Will SoBeck survive?

Read Book Two of the duet, *Becks*, coming VERY soon.

Acknowledgments

Writing a new book requires help from so many people I can't do without. I always try to include the people in here, but the moment it's printed, I realize I've left an important person off the list. Please don't hold it against me as I'm usually against a deadline, and my brain is drained.

First, I want to thank my wonderful husband, **Steve,** without him holding down the fort, none of my writing would be possible. Next, my kids help me in ways I can't possibly describe. They keep me sane, call me out on bullshit, and generally make me a happy person. So, thank you **Lacy and Kyle Hendricks** and **Teale Griffin**.

Next, thank you to my Beta readers. **Mayas Sanders, Teresa Talbot, Mary (my sister) Lefebvre, Stephanie Seay, and Julie Lafrance**. I can't move forward on anything without these ladies. They save me and keep me on track when my mind wants to wander off to chase butterflies or rock bands. I'm happy to call these ladies my friends as well as my helpers.

Julie Lafrance, my wonderful PA, uplifts me to the clouds, keeps me on track, and talks me off some ledges now and then. Thank you for all you do. I can never say this enough.

To the **Wander Squad, Wander Aguiar, Andrey Bahia, and Jenny Flores**. Thank you all for learning to love this old lady just like I am, even when you have to call me out on occasion. All of your friendship means the world to me.

To **Jamieson Fitzpatrick and Chris Correia** of CJC Photography for listening to my crazy and not complaining and for providing me with a lot of gorgeous pictures to inspire me.

KE Osborn, Leslie McAdam, and Michelle Mankin for friending me in a special way. Authors helping authors is the way it should be and having them to look over my shoulder some has made a huge difference.

To Swish Design, **Kaylene Osborn** and **Nicki Kuzn** for making making my book look and sound so beautiful. Thank you so very much. I couldn't do this without you.

To The **Finn's Freaks** Group, I thank those of you who faithfully read, visit, join takeovers, and talk. I appreciate you all in ways you'll never know.

This past year, I had the pleasure of joining a great group of authors and forming a fun group called **Sisters of Word Porn. Renee Harless, Teri Kay, Kristine Dugger, and Nichole Dennis.** We laugh, share naughty things, and rant when we need to, and they still love me. Thanks, Sisters!

Playlist

Check these out on Spotify or ITunes, AltRock Lives!

I love Alterative Rock Music. You never know what kind of sounds you're going to be introduced to. I listen to AltNation on Sirius Radio most of the time, but your local altrock stations are just as good. Check them out sometime.

I Would Die For You by **Matt Walters**
Sit Next To Me by **Foster the People**
Dangerous Night by **Thirty Seconds to Mars**
&Run by **Sir Sly**
Can We Hang On by **Cold War Kids**
Quarter Past Midnight by **Bastille**
Broken by Lovely **The Band**
Give Yourself a Try by **1975**
Burn Down the House by **AJR**

Thia Finn

Gold Rush by **Death Cab For Cutie**
Hunger by **Florence and The Machines**
Simplify by **Young the Giant**
Next to Me by **Imagine Dragons**
Thought Contagion by **Muse**
I Run To You by **Missio**

Goodreads Links
Check out the books below and add to your TBR list.

Assured Distraction Series
Assure Her (Assured Distraction Book One) – Keeton's Story

His Distraction Assurance Distraction Book Two) – Ryan's Story

His Assurance (Assured Distraction Book Three) – Gunner's Story

Distracted No More (Assured Distraction Book Four) – Carter's Story

Hayden's Timbre (Companion Book to Assured Distraction Series) Hayden's Story

Fat Boys Series
Half sac
Lateral Moves

Thia Finn

Website
http://www.thiafinn.com

Email
author@thiafinn.com

Facebook
https://www.facebook.com/ThiaFinn/?fref=ts

Goodreads
https://www.goodreads.com/author/show/
14206242.Thia_Finn

BookBub
https://www.bookbub.com/profile/thia-finn

About the Author

Growing up in a small town Texas, **Thia Finn** discovered life outside of it by attending The University of Texas, only to return home and marry her high-school sweetheart. They raised two successful and beautiful daughters while she taught middle school Language Arts and eventually became a middle school librarian. After thirty-four years, she retired to do her favorite things like travel, spend time off-roading with family and friends, hanging out at the Frio River, reading, and writing.

She currently lives in the same small town where she grew up with her husband and their new Chihuahua puppy, Josie. She can often be found stalking on social media, watching Outlanders, Game of Thrones, and the newest Netflix and HULU dramas.

Made in the USA
Coppell, TX
05 October 2023